P9-AGA-078

HER AND ME AND YOU

Also by Lauren Strasnick

Nothing Like You

HER AND ME AND YOU

Lauren Strasnick

SIMON PULSE
NEW YORK LONDON TORONTO SYDNEY

SIMON PULSE
An imprint of Simon & Schuster Children's Publishing Division
1230 Avenue of the Americas, New York, NY 10020
First Simon Pulse hardcover edition October 2010

For information about special discounts for bulk purchases, please contact
Simon & Schuster Special Sales at 1-866-506-1949 or business@simonandschuster.com.
The Simon & Schuster Speakers Bureau can bring authors to your live event.
For more information or to book an event contact the Simon & Schuster Speakers Bureau at
1-866-248-3049 or visit our website at www.simonspeakers.com.
Designed by Mike Rosamilia
The text of this book was set in Adobe Garamond.
Manufactured in the United States of America
2 4 6 8 10 9 7 5 3 1
Library of Congress Cataloging-in-Publication Data
Strasnick, Lauren.
Her and me and you / by Lauren Strasnick. — 1st Simon Pulse hardcover
ed. p. cm.
Summary: Struggling with family problems but determined to make new friends after moving and missing Evie her best friend since childhood, Alex is attracted to Fred and he to her despite the jealous meddling of Fred's twin sister, Adina.
ISBN 978-1-4169-8266-1 (hardcover : alk. paper)
[1. Coming of age—Fiction. 2. Family problems—Fiction.
3. Interpersonal relations—Fiction. 4. Brothers and sisters—Fiction.
5. Twins—Fiction. 6. Sex—Fiction. 7. Best friends—Fiction.] I. Title.
PZ7.S89787He 2010
[Fic]—dc22
2010007188
ISBN 978-1-4424-0949-1 (eBook)

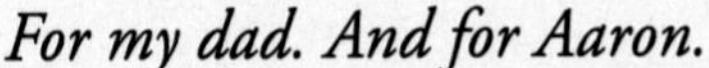

For my dad. And for Aaron.

HER AND ME AND YOU

1.

I met Fred first.

At a party on Orchard Ave. that Charlotte Kincaid took me to.

Him: "Need a beer?"

Me: "I've already got one."

"Well, drink up," he instructed. He was pale and skinny (and who wears Docksiders and corduroy?). "When you're ready I'll get you another."

Charlotte and I stood shoulder to shoulder chomping pretzels and watching the drunk crowd rock. Charlotte nursed her canned Bud Light and I picked at a pebble of salt wedged between my two front teeth.

"You're new," he said.

"Right." *You're new.* No question mark.

I'd been in Meadow Marsh a week. I missed home. And

Evie. And Charlotte Kincaid would never be Evie. She was soft-spoken and smelled like baby powder and dryer sheets. She had none of Evie's charm or spark.

"Let's sit," Fred suggested.

"I'd rather not."

Charlotte shot me a look, then wandered away. Where was she going? Bathroom? Food foraging? "I want to be alone," I told him, downing the rest of my beer and grabbing another out of the six-pack on the floor by his feet.

"You're at a party."

I felt my face flush, then twisted the top off the bottle and shoved the cap in my coat pocket.

"You don't really want to be alone. . . ."

True. I wanted to be with Evie. Or home in Katonah with Mom and Dad watching crappy TV. I took a bitter swig of beer and handed the bottle back. "You want the rest?" It was time to go.

"Your backwash?"

"Nice meeting you," I said. I pulled my hat from my bag.

"Wait—you're leaving?"

"Do me a favor? If you see Charlotte Kincaid, tell her I walked home?"

"You can't walk—it's pitch-black and freezing."

"I'll be fine," I said. "My grandmother's place is like, half a mile away."

"You live with your grandma?"

In fact, no. Grams was dead. But I'd just moved twenty-eight miles with my unhinged mother to my grandmother's place in Connecticut. Because my favorite parent, Dad, had done some very bad things with a paralegal named Caroline.

"Hey—"

I pulled on my hat and headed for the door.

"Wait!"

"What?"

"Your name?"

"Alex."

Alex, he mouthed. "I'm Fred."

"Fred, right." I was walking backward now, toward the foyer. "What's with the Docksiders, Fred?"

He looked down, then back up. "You don't like my shoes?"

I smiled, turned, and reached for the door.

2.

My mother was on her back—drunk, messy, her head hanging off the side of the sofa.

"Shit, Mommy." I dropped my keys, my coat, and hoisted her head back onto the couch cushions. "Hey," I said, loudly shaking her shoulders. I checked her pulse, her breath—still living. I grabbed an afghan off the recliner and covered her up, then rolled her onto her side just to be safe. I left a trash-can nearby.

In the morning, I called Evie.

"Yo."

"Hi." She sounded groggy; dreamy.

"You asleep?"

"Sort of."

"Well can you talk?"

A beat. I heard muffled whispering, laughing. Then: "I'll call you back."

"Eves?"

"What?"

"Is someone there?"

"I'll call you later." *Click.*

I chucked my cell onto the floor and the battery popped out. "Crap." I got out of bed, forced everything back in its place, jimmied the window open, and dialed Dad.

He picked up. "Snow."

"I know." I hammered the window open wider and stuck my head outside.

"How's my girl?"

"Freezing." I was inside now. Creeping back into bed. "How's home?"

"We miss you." We: Dad. Chicken, the dog.

"Mom's a real mess, you know."

"Honey."

"Have you broken things off with slutty Caroline?"

"Al."

"Because I'm ready for things to go back how they were."

"Honey, it's not that easy."

"I don't believe you," I said. Then, "Gotta go." I flipped my phone shut and buried myself under piles of covers. I curled my knees to my chest, inspecting a scab on my big toe.

3.

I met Adina the following Monday.

Meadow Marsh High was triple the size of my old school. Stained glass. Brick. Science wing. Student center.

I ate lunch alone at an empty table near the restrooms. French fries and ranch. My fave. I crammed five skinny fries into my mouth and looked up. Hovering overhead? Docksider Fred. With a girl.

"Can we sit?"

The girl wore a tattered black dress with four teensy rosebuds embroidered at the collar. Over that she had on a men's tweed coat. She was frail and blond and made me feel oversize and mannish.

"Is this your girlfriend?" I asked.

They sat side by side and close. The girl pulled five clementines out of her book bag, frowning. "His sister."

"Adina," said Fred, pulling a wad of green gum from his mouth. "Where's your friend?"

"Who?"

"That girl from the party."

"Oh." I shrugged. "Charlotte Kincaid. Yeah, I dunno."

"Orange?" offered Adina, digging her thumbnail into a clementine rind.

"No. Thanks though."

Fred pulled a to-go bowl of Cheerios from his blazer pocket. "Awesome table."

"Are you kidding?"

"Yes," he said, pulling the paper lid off his cereal bowl. "Seriously—next time, find a spot *away* from the bathrooms." He smiled. His freckled face made me want to bake a batch of brownies. Down a gallon of milk.

"Hey, what's your name?" The girl asked.

I redirected my gaze. "Alex."

"Alex." She chewed. "You're from . . . ?"

"Katonah."

"Oh, right." She nodded like she knew all about it. "So, Katonah, why are you here?"

"Ah—" I wasn't sure what to say. *My dad's a raging slut*? "My parents—Well, my dad—" I stopped, starting again: "My mom's from here," I finished.

"Fascinating," Adina deadpanned, angling away from me. "Eat faster," she said to Fred.

I winced, watching her nibble at an orange slice. Fred eyed me apologetically. "You settling in okay?"

I shrugged.

"If you need someone to show you around . . ."

Adina laughed, then slapped a hand over her mouth.

"What? What's so funny?" said Fred.

"No, it's just—" Who knew a giggle could sound so patronizing? "No, nothing. You're cute." She made her eyes into small slits.

"Well, if you're feeling lost," Fred said, ignoring her, ripping a piece of loose-leaf from his binder and scribbling something down. "My number." He smiled, sliding the paper forward.

"Thanks," I said cautiously, watching Adina. She watched me back. "Hey," I said softly. "Who's older?"

Fred took one last bite of cereal and pushed his bowl forward. "We're twins."

"Oh." They looked only vaguely alike. Both blond. Both thin. I wondered briefly what Evie might think of Adina. She'd love her pointy collarbone but would call her names behind her back. *Skeletor. Bobblehead.*

"Hey, Katonah."

"Yeah?"

"Here." She tossed a clementine rind across the table. It landed lightly in my lap.

"What's this for?" I picked it up, inspecting it.

"I just felt like giving you something."

"I'm touched?"

"You should be. Those things are precious. You think oranges grow on trees?"

4.

"Mommy, it's three. Have you been downstairs yet?"

The room was a dull black. I pushed back the curtains and cracked the window halfway.

"How was school?"

"Fine."

"Meet anyone nice?"

I sat down on the edge of the bed. "I don't know yet." I shut one eye against the light and watched Mom pull her hair into a tight knot. She used to be pretty. Now she looked worn and pale.

"Did Charlotte show you around?" My mother knew Charlotte Kincaid. She was the daughter of Deirdre Kincaid, Mommy's oldest friend.

"Sort of."

"Nice girl, right?"

I shrugged.

I could've stayed in Katonah. I *would've* stayed, had I thought my mother could survive the additional blow of me choosing Dad over her. "Come downstairs? I'll make you a snack."

She smiled. "Have you talked to Dad?"

I nodded. "I'm home with him this weekend."

Her face fell. She loved Dad, but Dad loved Caroline. I pushed back her covers and tried tugging her out of bed.

"No honey, not yet." She wasn't always this way. So screwy. Dad broke her. "Gimme a minute, okay?"

I let go and her hand hit the bed with a bounce.

5.

Weekend home.

Evie and I were dressed in big down parkas and galoshes. We lay on our backs in the snow.

"So wait—where was I?"

In the middle of telling me this: She'd found love. With a boy we'd known peripherally for years. Ben Ackerman. Curly hair. AP track. Water polo. He dated small, athletic girls. Cheerleaders, mostly. Girls who could be tossed in the air.

"At Pia Borelli's."

"Right, Pia Borelli's. So we left her house at eleven and went back to my place—"

"Where was Judith?" Judith: Evie's mother.

"Home. Downstairs watching CNN. And we were upstairs on the floor in my room playing cards and then, out of nowhere, he kissed me. I was like, 'Go fish,' and then we were kissing, and then . . ."

"And then what?"

"Then, you know."

"What?"

"We did it."

My heart plummeted. "Oh."

Evie's first kiss had happened when we were eleven. His name was Lennon and they dated for one week. She let him feel her up.

"You did it with Judith downstairs?"

"So?"

I'd never even kissed anyone. Except Evie. Who would sometimes use me for practice when she wanted to brush up on technique.

"No, nothing. It's just—well, what was it like?"

"Amazing."

"It didn't hurt?"

"*Yeah* it hurt, but you can't imagine how awesome it feels being that close to another human being." Evie was on her side, her wavy hair poking out in jagged tufts from underneath her cap.

"No, I can. I mean, I get it. Like, that person's inside you," I said.

"It's more than that." She sat up, pulled off her hat, and shook out her hair. "You just can't understand until you do it."

I flinched—"Oh, sure"—and nodded like that meant something. Evie had always been rash, a little reckless. But this—this took "impulsive" to a whole other level. "You really like him?"

"Why would you ask that? Of course." Her eyes narrowed. "Are you jealous?"

I wanted to hit her. Suddenly. Smack both her rosy cheeks and pound my fists into the powdery snow.

"Oh, don't look so glum," she said.

Did I look glum? I felt furious. Everything had changed so fast. Dad, Mom, Evie. Especially Evie. Why Ben Ackerman? Why now? Was she *that* eager to leave me behind? "One day I'll get it I guess."

"No," she whimpered, locking an arm around my neck. "You will stay this way forever. Pure and virginal." She pulled back. "It suits you."

I shook Evie off and sat upright. "What if I don't want to stay this way?"

She wrapped her arms around my body, pulling me into a snug embrace. "I love you just as you are. Why is that bad?"

"So you get to grow up and I don't?"

"That's not what I meant." Evie tightened her grip. "Why aren't you hugging me back?"

I lifted my arms, hugging back. "Better?"

"Yes," she said, squeezing the crap out of me. "Much."

* * *

Dad made four-cheese lasagna for dinner. Salad. Good crusty bread and butter. Apple pie for dessert. He even let Evie and I down half a bottle of red. I like nothing more than binge-eating with loved ones—but this meal felt shockingly bad. Spoonfuls of Caroline, my broken mother, my philandering Dad. A dash of Ben Ackerman for added richness and flavor.

"Al, you're not eating."

"I'm drinking," I said, raising my cup. Evie laughed. Her lips were purple.

"You want something else? Plain pasta? It'll take me two seconds to make—"

"I'm not really hungry." I pouted, jabbing a mound of arugula with my fork. My dad smiled, his brow wrinkling. He shoved a huge piece of sauce-slathered bread into his mouth. He chewed. His chewing drove me crazy. Everything I'd once loved—his sheepish posture, his glasses, his bald spot and dorky humor—all of it, now, drove me up-the-wall nuts.

"I'm going upstairs." I stood, facing Evie. "You coming?"

She flashed a desperate look at my dad.

"Al, come on, stay down here." He looked so sad. "We don't get to do this too often anymore."

"Right, I know." I glared at him sideways and shoveled two messy slices of pie onto my dinner plate. "Not my fault." I shrugged. I looked back at Evie: "Yes or no? You coming?"

"Yes." She dusted some crumbs off her lap. "Right behind you," she said, glancing back at my dad.

* * *

After the apple pie and wine, we lay on our backs on my bed, our bellies distended and our lips stained red.

"Watch this." Evie said, sitting up and, groaning, pulling my laptop off the desk and onto the bed. Kitten videos. Kittens stuck in boxes. Kittens taking baths. We laughed. We watched video after video, hysterical. We laughed so hard our insides hurt.

"Why'd you have to go?" Evie asked, rolling onto her side; catching her breath.

"Oh, Eves, come on. I'm right here."

"Right now you are." She sat up. "I see you, what, twice a month now?" She frowned. "You could've stayed."

"No way," I said, slamming my computer shut. "Liz is a complete wreck."

She stuck her thumb in her mouth and nibbled on a hangnail.

"Besides," I continued, "you've got that guy now. Ben. You don't need me."

"That's different."

"No it's not."

"It is," she insisted. "Don't be stupid. He's a boy."

"So?"

"So it's not the same thing."

I shrugged. I doubted I'd ever love anyone the way that I loved her. I couldn't imagine making new friends, let alone loving a boy. "Why'd you hang up on me last week?"

"When?"

"Last week when I called. You were with him, weren't you?"

"I don't remember," she said. But that was a lie, she did remember. She bit down harder on her thumbnail.

"Why don't you come visit," I suggested.

"When?"

"Next weekend?"

"Ben has a meet." She blinked. "I said I'd go."

"Right."

She reached for my hand, taking hold, squeezing tight. "You should come."

"Oh, I don't know . . ." I said, as if I had friends, commitments, *a life*. "Maybe," I said. "I'll let you know how my schedule shapes up."

6.

If Evie could love someone else, so could I.

Charlotte Kincaid and Libby O'Neil set their trays down at their regular spot by the coffee cart. I waited by the vending machines and watched them sip milk, pop open two bags of chips, and drop napkins on their laps.

"Hey," I said, jogging toward their table. "Hey, hi." I stopped, smiled, and dropped my bag on an empty chair. "Sorry about the other night."

Libby eyed me.

"I told that guy Fred to tell you I was leaving."

"Which guy?"

I scanned the cafeteria for Fred and spotted him and Adina four tables over.

"That guy," I said, watching Fred watch me. Charlotte and Libby turned to look. He saluted.

"Fred Bishop?" said Charlotte.

I nodded. "He didn't tell you I'd left?" She shook her head. I babbled on: "I just, I felt kind of sick and claustrophobic and didn't know where you were—"

"Sit down, Alex."

"Oh." I nodded. "Yeah, okay." I sat, pulled an apple and a small plastic bag of Triscuits from my knapsack. *Friends. Look how easy.*

"So, Alex."

"Yeah?"

Libby's face was blank. "How are your classes?"

"Fine." I nibbled a cracker and watched the twins while I talked. "I like my world lit."

"Who do you have?"

"Kordova."

Adina and Fred read novels and picked at their packed lunches.

"Getting to know the Bishop twins?"

I darted my eyes back to Libby. "Oh. I guess."

"I mean, you're new, so you should know: People don't like them."

I felt instantly, inexplicably defensive. "Why's that?"

"Why? Because Adina Bishop is a creepy anorexic who is completely obsessed with her brother." She unwrapped a single square of pink pillowy bubble gum and set it on her tongue. "It's sick. They're like, in love with each other."

I laughed. "Oh, come on."

She blew a bubble. Then a bubble inside a bubble.

"He dated this girl once," Charlotte added. "Audrey Glick?"

I glanced quickly at the twins, then back at Charlotte's square stare. "Yeah?"

"She doesn't go here anymore. She transferred to Sacred Heart in Brooksville."

"So?"

"So, you don't think that's weird?"

"You guys are funny," I said, straightening up. I ate another Triscuit. Watched Adina and Fred flip pages and snack on cute foods like berries and ladyfingers. "I have to read for next block," I said, pulling a beaten copy of *The Odyssey* from my backpack. "You guys mind?"

They shook their heads. "Go ahead," they said. They didn't mind at all.

After that.

Fred dumped his lunch scraps and packed up his books. I hovered nearby. "Hi," I said. He was alone.

"That Charlotte Kincaid. She's fun, right?"

I smiled. "Right."

We watched each other for a bit. "Nice sneaks."

I looked at my feet, dressed in white canvas Keds. "Very fashion-forward. So old they're new."

Fred laughed.

"You again." She came out of nowhere, wiping damp hands against her silk blouse.

"Me, yep." I straightened up. "How are things?"

Adina ignored the question, grabbed her coat off the back of her chair. She looked at Fred. "You ready?"

He tugged on his blazer lapels and stepped toward me. "What do you have now?"

"French."

"Walk with us?" He pointed left. "We're going this way."

"You two have class together?"

"No," Adina snapped.

I looked pleadingly at Fred. I couldn't help myself. I'd never met someone so standoffish and cool.

He smiled sympathetically, talking on. "I've got world lit. Adina's free this block."

She stopped, exhaled dramatically, and fluffed her skirt. "Okay, I'm going."

"Where?"

"Outside. You guys . . . *stroll.*" She pulled on her jacket and marched heavily toward the exit.

"Wow."

"Just—" Fred raised a hand, waiting, watching Adina go. "It's not personal."

"You're sure?"

"Yeah, yes. This is how she is. She's—" He shook his head, inhaling deep. "Not good with new people."

"Oh."

We stood for a bit.

"What're you doing later?"

"Later?"

"Yeah. Wanna come by after school?"

I laughed.

"I'm serious. We've got big dinner plans. Potato samosas. Chutney from scratch."

"You're kidding."

"I'm not."

"Seriously? Your sister *hates* me."

"She doesn't, I swear. She's actually really great." He touched my arm, then quickly retracted his hand. "Come."

If Evie could love someone else, so could I.

"Chutney from scratch?"

Fred grinned. "From scratch, yes. I'm telling you. The girl can cook."

7.

The house was huge. Stone. Creeping ivy. Small, murky, lily pad pond out front; glass greenhouse in the back. Inside, it was dark and messy and smelled like pipe tobacco and stale pretzels.

We sat on high stools in the middle of the kitchen, peeling potatoes and shelling peas for Adina's samosas.

"Something about raw peas . . ." she said, turning her nose up, leaning across the island while rolling a pea between her fingertips. "Here," she said, pressing the small, green ball against my lips. "Eat it."

I ate the pea. It was crunchy and tasted like grass. I eyed Adina. She'd been maniacally upbeat since I'd arrived. Friendly. Welcoming. As if she'd been switched with some amiable doppelgänger.

"Good, right?"

"Mm."

Fred finished another potato and chucked it across the countertop at Adina. She backed up. "What? What's your problem?"

"Is this it? How many more do you need?"

"I need four."

"You have four." Fred stood, pulling a cigarette from behind his ear. He bit the tip.

"Oh no, please don't," I pleaded.

"What's the problem?"

Dad smoked when I was a kid. The smell triggered nostalgia and queasiness. "So gross."

"No, but tell me how you really feel." He yanked the cigarette from his lips and tossed it onto the countertop. "Better?"

"Much."

"You want the tour?"

I looked to Adina, still shelling peas.

"Go ahead," she said, pushing her hair back with the heel of her hand. "Shoo." She grabbed a bowl from the cupboard and a potato ricer off the drying rack. "I've got potatoes to mash."

Upstairs was brighter than downstairs. I followed Fred. First, Adina's room, where every square inch of the floor was covered with books, clothing, old dolls, and broken CD cases; her walls plastered with cutouts, drawings, dried flowers, and macaroni art. Even her bed was hard to spot. "Impressive, right?" Fred looked at me. "She doesn't sleep here."

"Where does she sleep?"

"Depends. Guest bed. Couch. In the summer sometimes she'll pitch a tent and sleep outside."

"No shit."

"No, really."

Next up: his room. More books, thrift store paintings, records, stereo equipment, packs of tobacco, and rolling papers—but all of it arranged in neat little piles around the room.

"You're a minimalist."

He laughed and picked a tiny gray kitten up off the rug. "This is Egg Roll." He passed me the cat. Its bony body squirmed in my arms.

"There's another one."

"Where?"

"Somewhere. Downstairs, maybe? Called Banana." He grabbed my elbow and a crazy current rolled up my arm. "Come on, let's look."

Later, we ate Adina's dinner on the floor of the drained indoor pool. We sat on blankets over pool tiles. "Why no water?" I asked, taking a big bite of fried potatoey goodness.

"Upkeep," said Fred.

I nodded like I understood what that meant. "Parents?"

"In the Dominican. Our Dad. Just this week, though."

"Dead mom," said Adina, chomping a pea.

"I'm so sorry."

She gripped the wine bottle between her legs and yanked out the cork. "Fuzzy memory," she said with a shrug. "She died when we were kids." She took a sip from the bottle and passed it on.

"How long have you lived here?" I asked.

"All our lives," she said. Then: "You must miss home."

"I do."

"You like Meadow Marsh?"

"Not really." I took a quick swig of wine. "I can't get comfortable."

I looked at her plate. She'd sliced it all up, mashed the samosas and chutney together and spread it around, but as far as I could tell, she hadn't consumed an ounce of it.

"Stuffed," she said, noticing my glare.

"Sure," said Fred, leaning back.

We all lay back. That's when I noticed the mural: Two goats and a galaxy of yellow stars.

"Do you have a boyfriend?" Adina asked me.

"No."

She went on. "I've never been in love. Fred had a girlfriend once. Didn't you?"

"Yep."

"So clingy. . . ."

"Was not."

"Oh, come on. She was needy and clingy."

Fred sat up and sipped some wine. Adina continued. "Neediness. That's not love."

"Oh yeah?" said Fred. "What is?"

"Who knows," she moaned, rolling onto her side. Then: "Any ideas, Katonah?"

I shook my head. She smiled and looped her pinky through my belt loop. I looked down—half amused, half freaked out. "I think it's just one of those things. . . ." she said. "Like, a know-it-when-you-see-it sort of situation." She pulled hard on the waistband of my jeans.

8.

"You look high. Are you high?"

The house was packed with people, and the music was so loud I could barely hear Evie's raspy voice over all that thumping base. "I drank too much, Al. Here. Hold this." She pressed a red plastic cup to my hand, then hooked her nails into the top of her tights and tugged upward.

This was Ben Ackerman's post-meet rager.

Yellow and black streamers (Katonah colors) were tied to the wall sconces, vanilla cake was smooshed into the living room rug, and a keg sat in a bucket of melting ice in the corner of the kitchen.

Evie sunk to the floor and pulled me down with her. "Let's sit," she said, resting her head on my shoulder.

"Hey, Eves? Let's go soon."

"Just a little longer, okay?"

I nodded. I was sober and severely bored.

"Want some?" She rattled a box of Junior Mints under my nose.

"Thanks, no."

"You sure?"

"Yeah. Yes."

She sleepily ate her candy. I closed my eyes and when I blinked back to life, Ben Ackerman was parked nearby. "Alex," he said, running a hand through a thick matte of brown curls. "Welcome home."

"Thanks much."

Evie reached up, grinning, tugging Ben to the floor. "Kiss me," she said, puckering up. He pulled Evie forward by her dress straps.

"I'm going to the bathroom," I said, standing, nauseated; hiding my eyes and heading off.

Back from the toilet, and Evie was gone. I did a quick sweep of the room, checked the kitchen, the keg line, the den—I even checked the mudroom off the foyer. Then, over the doggy gate and up the steps. There were three bedrooms. I picked one and pressed my ear to the door. Silence. So I asked a guy slumped on the floor in a fleece pullover if he'd seen Evie.

"Who?"

"Or Ben Ackerman?"

The guy pointed to the door at the end of the hall.

"Is he with a girl?"

"Yeah."

"With, like, wavy hair to here?" I held my hand to my chin.

He nodded.

"Thanks," I said, staring helplessly down the dark corridor. I could've knocked. Instead I plodded back downstairs, grabbed my coat and bag from behind a leather recliner in the den, and left the party.

At first, it felt great, breathing icy air, away from the crowds and music, even Evie. But seconds later, I just felt pissy and bad.

I skated to my car, sneakers sliding over slick, frozen pavement. Once inside, I waited. I ran the heat for a bit. Made a bed in the backseat. Read Evie's copy of *Gatsby* that she'd left on my dash. Then finally, around three, I conked out.

When I awoke, the sky was gray-blue and Evie was pounding both hands on the hood of my car. She made kissy faces at me through the foggy window.

"Open up!" she screamed. "Hurry! I'm freezing."

I leaned over and flipped the lock. Evie climbed into the backseat and linked her arm through mine. "Brrr," she squealed, wriggling around. "Hi."

No, I thought. *No happy wriggles.* "I slept in the car," I said.

She snuggled close. "You didn't have to wait."

"I can't go home, Evie. My Dad thinks I'm at your place."

"Well, thanks for waiting." She grinned. "Let's get egg sandwiches. Doesn't that sound good?"

I took a beat. "What were you doing in there?"

Evie laughed, pulled back, and looked at me. "What do you *think* I was doing?" She hoisted her leg over the armrest—"Come on. I'll drive"—and slid into the driver's-side seat. "You gonna stay back there forever?"

"I dunno. Maybe."

"What, you're pissed at me now? For real?" She turned the ignition.

I stayed in the back and buckled up.

"Fine. Stay there," she said, accelerating.

I put my nose to the icy window and watched colonial after colonial speed by. "Did you forget about me?" I asked.

"Don't be crazy."

"I'm here one night, Eves. I slept in the car."

"Since when are you so insanely uptight?"

"I'm sorry?"

"I mean, what's the big deal, Alex? We went to a party. I drank and hung out with my boyfriend. That's what people at parties do."

"So he's your boyfriend now?"

"Oh my God." She shifted the car into third, grinding my gears.

I winced. "Be careful, please."

"Leave it to you to make me feel guilty for being happy."

"Oh. Is that what I'm doing? I'm depriving you of your happiness?" I grabbed her headrest, pulling myself forward. "You *abandoned* me, Evie. I slept in my fucking *car*."

"Alex, you don't live here anymore." She was shaking; putting extra emphasis on each word. "What do you expect me to do? Not talk to anyone? Not have a life?"

I felt stung. Sudden shame. What *did* I expect? Without me, she had no one. I let go of the headrest. "You're right," I said. I should've been happy she had Ben. Why wasn't I happy? "I shouldn't have come."

"No, Al . . ."

"I knew you had plans with Ben. I'm like, the third wheel."

She shook her head. "Alex."

"No, I don't mean for that to sound shitty; I just, I crashed your party. Sorry."

"I wanted you here."

I believed her. She wanted us both. Me and Ben. We were just the wrong fit. "I'm tired, Eves." I collapsed sideways on the seat. "When we get back to your place, I'm going to grab my stuff and go."

"Alex, come on. Stay. We'll get breakfast." She paused, then said, "I'm sorry I yelled."

"No, it's fine." I shut my eyes. "I'm sorry too."

We drove for a bit. Evie switched on the radio. Then:

"We're passing Hugo's. Should I stop, Al? Egg sandwiches?"

"Oh, I dunno."

"You need to eat something."

I wanted the night to be over. Still: "All right," I mumbled, eyes shut. "Hugo's," I said, relenting. "They do a mean fried egg."

"They do," Evie said, perking up, parking. "Soft, but never runny."

9.

I slept the day away, got up at four, and stumbled downstairs. Mom was gone. I grabbed a bag of Fritos from the cabinet and put the kettle on for tea. I felt itchy and half-baked, crammed a handful of chips in my mouth, and picked an Earl Grey tea bag out of the tin next to the toaster. The kettle blew. I switched on the television, dumped scalding water in my cup, dug my cell out of my book bag, and dialed Fred.

"Hi," I said. "It's Alex."

"Alex." He sounded surprised.

"Listen, I—" I wasn't sure what I meant to say. I thought about it for a second or two, then came up with this: "I want to hang out."

"Oh. Okay."

"Now." I was eager to wash away yesterday.

"Right now?"

"Do you have plans?"

"Well, no. I mean, yeah, I'd love to do something. It'll just be me, though. Adina's out."

"That's fine." I racked my brain for an activity to suggest. Just us two. Milk shakes? Movie?

"How about the Audubon?" offered Fred. It was freezing out. Nearly dark. "Come on, you'll love it. Nature stroll."

I looked down at my nightgown. "I need to change."

"Half hour?"

"Okay." Then: "Wait, where?"

"Pemberwick and Holly. Off Route One?"

I parked, pulled the emergency break, and got out of the car. "Hi," I said, waving. He wore a tweed coat (I'd seen it before, on Adina), a burgundy scarf, and a pair of beaten, black Converse. I wore my big, ugly parka.

"Nice coat."

"Shut up."

We both smiled. He twirled his keys around one finger. "You ready?"

I nodded.

"This way," he said, tugging me past an iron gate, along a stone walkway that circled the perimeter of an educational center, and down an icy slope. We emptied out into proper Connecticut forest: skinny trees; soupy patches of old snow;

dead, matted grass. I grabbed the back of Fred's coat, suddenly freaked. Darkness. Woods.

He laughed. "You scared?"

I let go of his coat, stiffening. "I'm not scared."

"Adina and I used to come here a lot."

Why was I alone in the woods with a boy I barely knew? Was this how stuff happened? Was this how Ben Ackerman and Evie happened?

"You sure you're okay?"

"I'm fine."

"You look a little peaked."

"Do I?"

We walked on, ducking beneath low branches and sliding between bare brush. Crossing rocky streams and stone walls. "Are you cold?" he asked, grabbing my hands. "You are, you're freezing."

I pulled back. "My teeth are chattering. Listen." I relaxed my mouth and let my teeth clank together.

"Shit, Katonah. Let's go back."

"No, it's okay." I hugged myself. "I'll be all right."

"You're sure?"

This was my idea. I wanted friends. "Positive." I kept walking. "Tell me something."

"Like what?"

"Something you know that I don't."

He was two steps ahead. "The mountain laurel."

"What's that?"

"State flower."

I picked a branch off the ground and wedged it between my pointer and middle fingers like a cigarette.

"Hey, can I ask . . . ?" He grabbed on to a tree trunk, propelling himself forward.

"What?"

"You're here because . . . Why?"

"What do you mean?"

"I mean, you started mid-term."

He wanted specifics. The juicy details. "I came with my Mom."

"I know that part."

I stepped onto a rock and hopped off. "My dad had an affair," I said.

"Oh." He picked a twig off the ground. "Sorry."

"That's okay." *Dad. Affair.* "So that's why I'm here. Mid-year."

The path split. "Which way?" he asked.

"You don't know?"

"I mean, it's been a while." He looked at me. "Right or left?"

"Left?"

We kept on. Fred pulled a flashlight and tobacco pack from his coat pocket. "Will you kill me if I smoke?"

"Seriously? On our nature walk?"

"Is that a yes?"

"Don't." I ran two steps ahead. "It looks wrong on you."

"Oh yeah?"

I faced him. "You're way too sweet to smoke."

"Too *sweet*?"

"Yeah, dude. You've got freckles! And such nice skin! The cigarettes—they don't go."

He shook his head and kept walking. "Too sweet . . ."

I grabbed on to the arm of his tweed coat. "You're mad?"

"I mean, you just completely emasculated me, but no. Not exactly mad . . ."

I laughed. "Sorry."

"No sweat."

"No, seriously, stop walking."

He stopped.

"I shouldn't have said that. You want to smoke, go ahead."

"No, I mean, you're right. It's a shitty habit." He met my gaze and held it.

I looked away, feeling woozy and embarrassed. "Where are we, anyways?"

"I don't really know."

Lost. Frozen solid.

"Should we go back?"

We turned back. Fred's hand brushed my hand and my head got hot. "How much farther?" I asked. Evie's face was darting around my brain like a trapped black fly.

"Fifteen minutes, maybe?"

"Can I get the flashlight?" I asked, suddenly keen for an activity or task.

"Here," Fred said, pitching the light my way. "Knock yourself out."

10.

Thursday night.

I was watching a movie in bed with Mom when my cell rang.

"Hello?"

"Can you talk?"

Evie, I mouthed to my mother, standing up. "Yeah, I can talk."

We hadn't spoken since Sunday. Record breaking. We'd never gone that long before.

"Is stuff still weird?"

I tiptoed out the door, down the hall, to my room. "What stuff?"

"With us, I mean."

"Oh." I tensed up. "I don't know. Is it?" I lay down, covering up with an afghan.

"I mean, no, right?"

"Right," I said, my voice faltering. "We're fine."

"Good." She exhaled. "Because I need to tell you something."

I braced myself.

"It's about Ben."

Awesome. "What about him?"

She let go a hysterical squeal. "He loves me."

I felt an instant angry surge.

"Did you hear what I said?"

He loved her? How could he possibly love her? "Yeah." I sat up. "He actually *said* that? I mean, you've barely been together a month."

"I know, I know, right? But he said it and now . . . I dunno, it just *feels* right." She was gleeful; her voice high and happy.

"But what does that mean? It 'feels right'? You hardly know each other."

"We know each other."

"No, you don't. He doesn't *know* you."

"Alex," she snapped.

"What?" I pressed on. "Well did you say it back?"

"Yes."

"Why? Why would you do that?"

"Because I meant it, Alex." A beat and then, "Wow, I gotta go."

"Wait, *why*?"

"I thought I could talk to you."

"You can."

"I *can't*!" she shrieked. "Listen to you. 'He doesn't *know* you,'" she mimicked. "He *knows* me. He *loves* me."

My chest tightened. "Okay. He loves you." I took a breath. "I'm sorry."

"I don't believe you."

But I was, instantly regretful and sorry. "No, I mean it. I'm sorry, Eves."

"You said that last time. In the car. You said you were sorry and now it's the same shit all over again."

I clutched the afghan to my chest. "I'll make it up to you."

She took an exasperated breath. "Al, I gotta go."

"But why? Don't go yet."

"I have to. Judith needs me downstairs."

"But we're okay, right? You're not really mad, are you?"

"I gotta go, Al." She hung up the phone.

11.

Nighttime. Bishop pool.

Adina was on her side, picking at the runs in her tights and singing the chorus to a song I'd never heard. Fred was to my left, and every now and then he'd throw a cookie or a cracker crumb at my face. He'd say, "Chin up, Katonah," and I'd smile. I'd been like this for days. Missing Evie. Really blue.

"Eat one," Adina instructed, thrusting a cookie tin under my nose. I took a cookie and ate half. "Good?" she asked.

"Really good." They were gritty and sweet.

"Cornmeal," she said, sitting back. "My favorite."

"So have one," said Fred. He'd grabbed the tin from Adina and was rattling it around.

"I ate a bunch earlier."

"Sure you did."

They glared at each other. Adina broke the moment by

doing a coy little dance—shaking her shoulders and hiding behind her hair.

"You think you're cute?"

"I do."

"Come on, eat one."

"Why?"

"For me."

"For you?" She was laughing.

"Why is that funny?"

"Fred. It's a cookie. Relax."

"Well if it's *just a cookie* then what's the big deal?" He pulled one from the tin. "Stick it in your mouth and eat it."

She swatted the air. "Get that shit away from me."

"Hey, guys—" They ignored my interjection.

Fred shoved the tin and stood up.

"Wow." She waited till he'd gone, then said, "Boys."

Boys and their moody, food-phobic twin sisters. "You guys fight a lot?"

"A lot?" She cocked her head. "I don't know, I guess." Then, smiling: "We compete."

"Oh yeah?"

"For attention. Affection. You know." She glanced up. "You have brothers?"

"No. Just me."

"That's too bad."

"It's all right. I have a best friend. That I grew up with."

She looked perplexed. "How is that the same?"

I flinched. "No, it's just—we're close. And we fight. Like you guys."

"About?"

I leaned against the side of the pool. "I dunno. Her boyfriend."

"What about him?"

"I don't like him."

"Well maybe they won't stay together."

"Yeah, well, they love each other." I rolled my eyes.

Adina put a hand on my head, patting me. "There, there, Katonah. I'll be your friend."

"Will you?" Had Adina ever had a friend?

"Sure." She uncorked a bottle of wine—"Why not?"—and took a swig.

"Can I have some of that?"

She passed the bottle. "Hey, Katonah."

"Mm?" I took a slow sip, tilting my head back.

"You like my brother?"

I froze, mouth full, and righted myself.

"It's okay. You can tell me."

I swallowed. "I mean, of course, yeah. We're friends."

"No, I don't mean, like, are you *pals*. I mean, *do you like Fred?*"

Did I like Fred? I wasn't sure. Did Fred like me? "I mean, I don't think—it's not like that with me and him."

She relaxed. "Good. I mean, not that there's anything

wrong with liking him, it's just—he's a bad boyfriend. You'd be miserable."

I nodded like I understood whatever it was she was hinting at. Then, after a moment or two: "Well, wait, what do you mean?"

"I mean, that girl he was with? Audrey Glick?"

"Yeah."

"He wasn't faithful."

"Oh."

"I mean, he tried, he's just—he can be kind of compulsive."

"Compulsive?"

"He has, like, a problem." She was gesturing a ton with her hands. "He sleeps around. And then, like, lies about it."

"Oh." It took me a few seconds to process. "Wait, he lies?" Fred seemed so earnest and true.

"Don't tell him I told you."

"No, I won't, it's just—" I tried picturing Fred with a multitude of girls: preppies, sluts, brainiacs. Fred on top. Fred down below. Fred with a whip and a cigarette. I stifled a laugh. "Are you kidding?"

"*No*, I'm not kidding." Adina leaned forward. So close I could smell the Merlot on her breath. "You're too nice for him, Katonah."

I pulled back, stung.

Fred was jogging toward us now, carrying two huge jugs of water. "Okay, fuck the cookies—I don't care about the cookies. Water, anyone?" He was breathless, jovial.

"Alex and I finished the wine. Look." She flipped the empty bottle upside down, pouting.

"That's fine," he shrugged, sitting down. "Why would I care if you finished the wine?"

"I dunno," she said. "You're funny about things." She looked at me conspiratorially. "He's very territorial," she insisted. "He hates when I take his stuff."

12.

Morning.

I was jittery, nauseated, and eating spoonfuls of dry Grape Nuts straight from the box. Mom was next to me. We were watching PBS.

"So what did you guys do all night?"

"Nothing. Slept."

"That's it? Why couldn't you sleep at home?"

"We did other stuff too. Built a fort. Ate cookies."

"All night?"

I dropped my spoon. "I dunno, Mommy. *Yes*, all night."

"Al, hey."

"What?"

She made her eyes wide. "Watch it."

"Watch what?" I was hungover. Short on patience.

"The attitude," my mother snapped.

"Oh, okay," I said. "What, three seconds of sobriety and you think you get to reprimand me for a coed sleepover?"

She slapped me hard across the face.

I watched the floor, stunned.

"Oh God, oh God, Al, I'm sorry. I'm so sorry." Now she was clutching me, hugging me, tearing up. "You didn't deserve that, I'm so sorry."

I touched my cheek, reeling, letting her sob and grab at me. "It's fine," I said, pulling back, dazed, shaken. I wasn't sure whether to laugh or cry. I'd never been slapped before.

"Honey. It's not you. You're a good girl."

She wept. She put her head in her hands and she cried.

"Mommy, it's okay. I know you didn't mean it."

"I'm just a little sad this morning, baby. I don't mean to take it out on you."

"It's fine," I said, rubbing her back, feeling a mix of resentment and pity. "Really," I insisted. My mind flashed to Fred. "I'm okay."

13.

I was in line for hard-shell tacos. The kind with ground beef, shredded lettuce, and plastic cheese. The lunch lady passed me a plate over the Plexiglas divider. I got in the cashier line behind Charlotte Kincaid.

"Hi," I said.

Charlotte smiled stiffly, then turned toward the register. Icy. Aloof. But understandable. I was her fair-weather friend.

"Can I sit with you guys today?"

She pulled four crumpled bucks from her pocket and looked at me over her shoulder. "Are you talking to me?"

Charlotte had what seemed like a limitless reserve of Bishop information. "Yeah, of course." I'd been chasing her around all morning long.

"Well, what about your bosom friends?"

"I mean, they're around." I angled my head and caught

sight of Fred hovering intently over his cereal bowl. "I just—I actually wanted to ask you about them." I thought about what Adina had said: Fred was a liar, lothario, cheat. But really? The guy with the freckles and cereal obsession?

"Pay for your taco, please?" She waved me forward. "Libby's waiting."

I handed a ten to the cashier. "Adina just—she said something—" *Fred: XXX, "perplexing."*

"Big surprise."

"Something about Fred, being, like, a womanizer." I collected my change. "Is that true?"

Charlotte looked at me blankly. "How should I know?"

We were walking now. Across the cafeteria, toward Libby.

"Well, you said you knew stuff about him and that girl—"

"Audrey Glick?"

"Yeah."

"I mean, a little. But I don't know anyone else he's been with. I mean, *look* at the guy." She tossed a hand toward Fred. "Who would hook up with him?"

I blinked.

"There's Libby." She upped her pace. "Wait, so, why?"

"Why what?"

"Why do you care who Fred Bishop's been with?"

"I don't."

"You just said you did."

"No. I was telling you what Adina said. That he'd been with, like, *multiple* girls."

She stopped. Faced me. "You like him."

"No."

She paused, pressing her lips together. "I think you do."

I looked at Libby, who was waving.

"Kincaid!"

Charlotte turned. "Hold on." Then: "Alex."

"What?"

She shifted impatiently from leg to leg. "I mean, have your little crush, whatever, but, Fred Bishop?"

"What? What's wrong with Fred?"

"He couldn't even dump his own girlfriend. He had Adina do it for him." She lifted an eyebrow and wagged her finger in my face. "You're like, Audrey Two. . . ." She said, slinking away. "Can't wait to watch the insanity unfold."

14.

"This is weird, right?"

Dad. Dad said this. We were at a restaurant right outside Meadow Marsh, eating palak paneer, papadums, and naan.

"It's weird, yes." I had refused to go home for the weekend. Evie and I hadn't spoken for a week and Dad—Dad was, at best, a shitty stand-in for my drunk mother.

"Al." He reached for the chutney, accidentally knocking my hand. "What do you think about spending one weekend away with me next month? We could ski. Stowe? Black Mountain?"

I ignored the invite. No weekends away. No rewards for bad behavior. "You and Mom should go somewhere. Or even just, like, out. On a date."

Dad shifted in his chair. "Oh, Al."

"Well why not? She'd like that."

"Al, honey, come on."

"You were married nineteen years, now what, you can't spend three seconds in the same room together?"

"Honey—"

"What?" He didn't say anything else so I pushed on. "How's Caroline?"

"Good."

"Awesome. You know, Mom's still pret-ty messy."

He dropped his fork. "You're mad, and you have a right to be mad, but Mom and I had issues way before Caroline came along—"

"Okay."

"Al—"

"Okay. Enough." I threw my hands up in quick surrender. "I don't want to talk about Caroline anymore. All right? I'm sorry I brought it up."

Dad cut the engine on Grams's gravel driveway, pulled the emergency break, and got out of the car.

Mom was waiting on the porch steps. She wore Grams's winter coat over a thin, sleeveless nightgown. It was freezing out. She looked ridiculous. Hungover, sleepy, and sexed-up.

"Babe." She kissed my cheek, looking past me, at Dad. "Go inside, okay? I'll be up in a bit."

From my bedroom window I watched. My view, perfect, if I leaned out the window and a little to my left.

Dad made a joke, gesturing broadly. Mom laughed, then cried. She put her head on Dad's chest. He touched her shoulder, she touched his shirt, and within seconds they were kissing. They kissed and they kissed and then Dad pulled away. "Liz," he said, and Mom wailed. She screamed and cried and kissed him again.

"Liz, stop."

I pulled away from the window.

The screen door slammed shut.

15.

Carbonara. *Anne Frank* on DVD. This was Bishop ritual.

"Which blanket?" I asked, digging through a wood trunk in the Bishops' downstairs guest room.

"The poofy one with the ducks," hollered Adina, poking her head through the door. "That one, yeah." She was balancing three steaming bowls of spaghetti. "Hurry up. Movie's starting."

I tugged on the tattered, faded duvet and followed Adina into the den. Fred was on the floor fluffing pillows. Credits rolled on a tiny TV. Dreamy music. Seagulls. Adina loved this movie. The old version—the black-and-white one. She said despite the ending, she found the story comforting. She liked the idea of being locked away.

We huddled together in front of the sofa. Adina took

small bites of carbonara and yanked the comforter up to her chin.

"Is your dad back yet?" I asked.

Egg Roll hopped onto Fred's lap. "Yeah." Adina fed him a strand of spaghetti from her bowl.

I looked around. "He's here?"

"He's working." Fred said.

"Tonight?"

Adina paused the movie. "Katonah, don't talk."

"Oh. Sorry—"

"You talk and it wrecks the mood."

I put down my bowl of pasta.

"Hey," said Fred. "No big deal."

Adina shot him a look. "It *is* a big deal. It's tradition."

"It's fine."

"It not."

"It's a fucking *movie*, Adina, chill out."

"Hey," I said, "I'm really sorry—"

"Don't tell me to chill out. And it's not just a movie. It's *our* thing."

"Adina," I said again.

She whipped around. "*What*?" Her cheeks were flushed and her eyes were wet.

"I can go."

She paused, considering my offer.

"You're not going," Fred said, putting a hand on my thigh.

Adina glanced down, to where Fred's fingers lingered, right above my kneecap. "Hey, D," Fred said. "Apologize."

She looked at me, her mouth settling into a thin, hard line. "I didn't mean you weren't welcome," she said.

"No, I get it," I said. "I'll shut up."

She smiled then, a small smile. "It's just really great, the movie." She sat back, rubbed one eye, and smeared her mascara. "But if you talk you miss all the good parts."

Fred moved his hand. I glanced quickly at him, then back to Adina.

"Finish your pasta," she instructed, her mood leveling off. "It's fine," she said, making gosh-golly eyes at Fred. "Fight's over." She picked up the remote and aimed it at the television. "Any last words before we restart the show?"

16.

"So, stuff's okay?"

Evie hadn't called me in a week and a half. "I mean, yeah, stuff's great, why?"

"What do you mean, *why*?" I'd called her.

"No, nothing, I don't know." She exhaled. "What's up with you?"

"Nothing. School. Liz. I've been over at the Bishops' a lot lately." I stuck a hand under my mattress and mashed my face to the bed.

"The Bishops?"

"You know. Fred. Adina."

"I don't."

"The twins? Oh, Eves, you'd freak. Their house is huge and they barely have parents and Fred dresses like a"—I laughed—"*hot* old man and Adina eats, like, air, I swear. She's a twig, you'd hate her. But actually, maybe you'd love her." I waited for Evie's response. Dead air. "Eves?"

"What?"

"Are you listening?"

"Sorry. The twins."

"You okay?" I wondered what she'd done all week. If she'd been miserable like me. "How's Ben?"

"Fine."

"Stuff's still good?"

"Why would you ask me that?" Her voice had an edge.

"I don't—" I stopped. Had I screwed up? "I called because I missed you." Then, quickly: "You're gonna stay mad forever?"

"I'm not mad."

"You are."

"I'm not, Alex, I'm really not." She sounded so tired. "I just don't know what to say right now."

"Why not?"

"I don't know. Stuff's different. Don't you think?"

"With us?" I took three short, hysterical breaths.

"Are you crying?"

I was.

"Please don't cry."

I couldn't stop.

"Please, Al, you're making me feel guilty."

I wondered how everything had changed so fast. At the

start of the year, Evie was my world. Mom and Dad were together. I had a dog. "I'm sorry I called."

"Don't be like that."

I wiped my nose on my sleeve. "Well how do you want me to be?"

"I don't know. Don't be upset."

"I can't help it."

"Al."

"Yeah?"

"Take a breath."

"Why?"

"It'll calm you down. Come on, inhale deep—"

I did.

"—and hold it."

17.

I spent most of my free period outside, high up, legs dangling off the edge of the brick wall by the science wing. Twenty minutes spent catching up on leftover lit reading; the other twenty, obsessively moping over Evie. I'd been trying to pinpoint the exact moment things went wrong with us—me leaving Katonah? Evie uniting with Ben? My lackluster reaction to their scorching affair?—when Fred approached carrying a small paper sack.

"Hey, Polar Bear." He tossed me the bag, then scaled the wall. "Aren't you cold?"

I nodded, thrilled to see him.

"For you," he said, gesturing to the sack, settling in.

"What's this?"

"Open it."

I looked inside. Chocolate. Heaps of black, glossy, misshapen chocolate.

"They're caramels."

I pulled two from the bag, grinning. "Here," I said, handing him one. I ate the other. Sweet, sticky, bitter. "Oh wow."

"Right?"

"No, these are, like, amazing."

He watched me. I touched my lips, covering up. "Don't stare," I said, chewing, beaming. "How'd I get so lucky?"

He looked away. "I just . . . felt like giving you something."

"You sound like Adina."

"Do I?"

"You talk alike," I said. Fred's head was cocked. I flashed on him kissing loads of girls: girls from my lit class, girls from my old school, Audrey Glick, Anne Frank. Fred with . . . "Anyways." Fred with *me*. "Thanks. A lot."

"Don't thank me." He ate his caramel. "Can I look at you now, or no?"

"Wait." I wiped my top lip. "Sure."

He glanced up. Smiled. "So."

"Mm?"

"Speaking of Adina . . ."

"Oh. Yeah. The other night, right?" Humiliating.

"I'm so sorry about that."

"No," I stuck my tongue between two molars, trying to loosen a bit of stuck caramel. "I mean, that's fine. I'm over it."

"You did nothing wrong. You know that, right?"

I shrugged. "I do that sometimes—talk too much?"

"No, you don't."

I pulled another caramel from the bag and handed it to Fred.

"Thanks." He squished it between his thumb and pointer finger. "She's just—" *Anorexic and moody? A liar? A saint? In love? In crisis?* "She's got a lot going on."

"Oh yeah?"

He popped his second caramel, continuing, "I mean, she's *amazing*." He looked at me. "Really loyal." Then looked away. "She's just—she's got some shit she's working on."

I tried to catch his eye again. "Like what? What's she working on?"

"I don't mean anything *specific*, just *issues*. Everyone's got shit they're not proud of. Don't you?" He looked up, finally. "Or are you perfect?"

"Yes," I said mindlessly. "Perfect."

He smiled. "Thought so." He ran his tongue over his left incisor. Then: "Will I see you later?"

"You're going?"

"I just wanted to give you those." He gestured to the brown paper bag. "You have plans later on?" He hopped off the wall.

"Nope."

"Wanna walk to Chester Hill? Get sandwiches?"

"*Bagel* sandwiches?"

Fred laughed and looked at me crooked.

"What?" I said, feeling psychotically giddy. "I like bagels."

"Three fifteen?" He was jogging backward toward the building. "Meet here?"

"Three fifteen." Then, "Wait, Fred!" I hollered, waving one tacky hand. He stopped, treading air. "Thanks again." I shook the bag.

"Anytime," he said, saluting. He reached for the door.

One forty-five p.m. Between blocks.

Adina grabbed me on my way to world lit. "Katonah—"

"Hey!" The promise of bagels. I was still maniacally peppy.

"Your jeans."

I glanced down. Adina was on her knees now, wiggling her finger through a tiny tear at my knee. "They're holey."

"I know."

She stood up, squinting. "You never wear dresses."

"I've got one."

"I'm going to Goodwill after school," she said.

"Oh, uh-huh."

"I'm going to look for something lacy. Wanna come?" She poked at a smear of dried paint on my thigh. "I'll buy."

I laughed, flattered and a little afraid. Alone time with Adina? She'd either cuddle me or kill me. *Tempting, but . . .* "I would, I'd love to—but I've got plans. With your brother, actually."

"Plans with Fred?"

"Yeah."

"*Today?*"

"Mmhmm."

She looked pale and pissed, so I said, "You should come," but didn't mean it.

"I can't." She grimaced. "I just told you. *Goodwill.*"

Okey-doke. "I'm gonna be late," I said, pointing down the hall, toward lit. "What about this weekend?" I asked, making up.

"What *about* this weekend?" She curtsied and did a little pivot, heading off.

I waited till quarter to four. I waited by the wall, freezing and swearing and scanning the courtyard for Fred. I jumped in place to keep warm, checked my watch twenty times, tried Fred's phone twice (direct to voicemail), then circled the building, hoping I'd been wrong about our plan. Had I misunderstood? *Should I check the bathrooms? The infirmary?* I ended up at my car, clutching my keys too tight and trying him one last time. "Hey," I started after the beep. "It's Alex. We were meeting at the wall, weren't we? By the science wing? It's ten till now, I'm headed home. If you get this, call me?"

18.

Deirdre Kincaid.

"Honey, pass the cheese, will you?"

Deirdre and Mom sat side by side, lapping up heaps of linguini and casserole. Charlotte was next to me, picking at her dinner.

"What is this?" Charlotte asked, cautiously nibbling at a forkful.

"It's a casserole," I said, annoyed, passing the bowl of grated parmesan to my mother. I'd spent an hour and a half salting, rinsing, assembling, baking.

"No, I mean, what's inside?"

"Tomatoes, ricotta, and eggplant."

"Tasty," Charlotte offered, taking a timid bite. She looked nothing like her mother, who was skinny, with short, sensible hair and glasses. Charlotte's hair was long and loopy. Her boobs were big. "Cook much?"

I dropped my fork.

"Alex makes really good banana pancakes. Right Al?"

I nodded at Mom. I was ready to break something. Charlotte's veiled insults, Fred's vanishing act—

"Char." Mom again. "Do you and Al see much of each other at school?"

"Alex spends most of her time with the Bishops."

"Oh, right! The twins."

"Hettie Whitmore's kids," Deirdre whispered.

"Oh." Mom nodded glumly, then sucked back some wine.

"Who's Hettie Whosiewhatsit?"

Deirdre smiled at me. "The mother. Hettie Bishop. Whitmore was her maiden name. Your mom and I went to school with her."

"She died, when? Ten, twelve years ago?"

I looked at the mush on my plate, picturing two lonely babes. I felt sad, then mad, remembering I'd been stood up. "Bathroom," I said, getting up. Time to check my phone. "Be back."

I darted up the steps to my room, bolting for my cell. One missed call. From Fred. I dialed back.

"Hey!"

"You're alive."

"Alex, I'm so sorry. I just got your message—"

"What happened to you?" I was panting from the run upstairs. "I waited till four."

"Adina got sick. She threw up last block and begged me to take her home."

"Oh," I said, relaxing slightly. A sick twin. "Is she okay?"

"Apparently. She's downstairs making gingersnaps."

Or not. "So . . . So why not call?"

"I did. I texted. Or, I had Adina text you from her phone on the drive. My cell died."

"I didn't get any text."

"I saw her send it."

"I didn't get any text," I repeated. I flashed back to Adina's pissy, pale face in the hallway at school. She hadn't looked sick to me. "She puked, huh?"

"Yeah." He paused. "I'm really sorry, Katonah. Seriously. I feel like an asshole."

"No, don't. It's okay," I said. I was relieved. I'd been screwed over, clearly, but not by Fred. "I have to go. The Kincaids are here."

"Who?"

"Charlotte Kincaid. And her mom." I sighed. "Charlotte's mom and my mom . . ."

"Right." He was silent for a bit. I pictured him with the phone wedged between his shoulder and ear, assembling a cigarette: a dusting of tobacco, one tight roll, a lick.

19.

Late afternoon. Dark already. Sitting on a towel in Grams's garage going through boxes of crap from Dad's house: old photos and books. Random kitchen equipment (a bread maker, a Cuisinart, a set of Cutco knives). Plastic containers stuffed with summer clothes, baby clothes, Mom's cream lace wedding dress. And found, in the back corner, between Mom's car and my bike, a box labeled ALEX, filled with diaries, yearbooks, letters from Evie. Folded notes written on loose-leaf. Who'd packed this up? Me? Mom? I picked a letter out and read the first few lines.

Hi. Can I copy off your worksheet? Can we bake something later on? A pie? A cake? A block of brie? Can we swim? Too cold or no? What's

```
Shapiro wearing? An ascot? What
the fuck's an ascot anyway? I crack
myself up.
```

"Hey."

"Hi." I'd called. I couldn't help myself. My heart was heavy with weepy nostalgia. "What're we doing?" I said.

"What do you mean?"

"I mean, come down. Eves, please?"

"Now?" she asked.

"No, I don't know. Next weekend, maybe?"

"I mean . . ."

"Eves, I'm in Grams's garage. I found all these letters."

"What letters?"

"In a Ziploc. Stuff from, like, Western and Eagle Hill." Junior high. Grade school.

"Well, what do they say?"

"I don't know, just—come down. We can look together."

She paused.

"You don't want to?"

"No, I do."

"You're sure?"

She took a quick breath. "I mean, I want to. I just—"

"What?"

"If I come, we're gonna fight."

"We won't."

"We might."

"No, we'll swear on it. Now, okay? No fighting."

"Promise?"

Easy. "Yes." Our troubles, done.

"Okay." Her voice was high now.

"Come Friday?"

"All right."

"Bring clothes for two nights."

"You're sure?"

"Mm. It'll be great. We'll do something fun."

"Meadow Marsh has fun?"

"Oh, barrels full," I joked. "They sell it by the crate on exit ramps off Ninety-Five."

20.

Ten a.m., Sunday.

Hovering in front of the fridge, shoveling yogurt into my mouth while searching the veg bin for something more—black banana? I grabbed it, then bumped the fridge shut with my hip.

Ding-dong, the bell. Seriously? Who was here? Mom was upstairs, asleep still. I slid across the floor in socks and tugged the door open. "Adina."

"Hi," she chirped. She was wearing a yellow peacoat, red lipstick, and had her hair pinned back in a wave. "Can I come in?" She rubbed her mittens together. "So cold!"

"I'm not dressed." I tried to block her view inside by spreading my arms wide.

"What're you doing?"

I dropped my hands, embarrassed. "Nothing. Come in," I said, stepping aside.

She pushed past me, stopping a few feet short of the plush plaid sofa. "Sweet."

I cringed. "It's my Grams's. Most of our stuff is still back in Katonah."

"Huh." She undid the top two buttons on her coat and took a seat.

"You want anything? Water?" *Why was she here?*

"Nope." She smiled. Sparkled. "I heard you never got my text."

"Oh."

"I got sick off a bad ham sandwich."

"Fred said."

"He told you about the sandwich?"

"Not the sandwich, no."

"Well I got sick right after I saw you."

"Mmhmm."

"You don't believe me?"

Well, Adina, you don't look like you eat sandwiches. "Sure."

She brightened. "Great. Get dressed. We'll go out."

I wasn't going anywhere. I had my whole day planned. Black banana, *Odyssey* essay, shitty Showtime movie marathon, ice cream dinner. "Where to?"

"Goodwill, *hello*. Clothes, remember?"

"Oh." I ran a hand over my holey sweats. In a minute I'd run upstairs and slip on my holey jeans.

"What? Why are you just standing there? Get ready," she

snapped. "If you're quick I'll buy you a coffee and croissant on the way."

"Is that padded?"

"Where?"

"The shoulders, come'ere." Adina curled her finger forward. "Yup," she said, jabbing around my collarbone. "Take it off." She spun around, pulling the dressing room curtain aside and going in search of something new. We'd been doing this for more than an hour. Dresses, blouses, corduroy pants. I peeled off the violet polyester. I had nothing else to change into.

"Here," Adina said, thrusting a sheer nightgown through the curtain gap.

"What is that?" I asked, inspecting it.

"It's for sleep. It's cute, right?" She wiggled it. "Try it on."

"It's see-through."

"So? You sleep in sweatpants. Come on, put it on. I want to see."

I obliged, slipping the thin fabric over my bra and underwear. I turned toward the mirror.

"Can I look?"

You could see everything. My belly button, beauty mark, my wide hips. Adina thrust the curtain aside. "Oh," she said, laughing. My palms got hot. I covered my breasts with my hands. "Oh, come on. Let me see." She stood next to me, gazing at my reflection in the full-length. "You look fine, you just—you have to take off your bra."

"What? *No.*"

"I'm kidding," she said. "God, you're so easy to freak out."

I winced. I felt fat and miserable. "This is pointless."

"What?"

"This. None of this stuff looks right." I ogled her tiny frame. Spindly and hollow. *Death chic.*

"It's all old crap, Katonah." Was that pity pursing her lips?

"You find clothes here."

"I have to dig," she said. She tugged on my hair. "Besides, no one would look good in that thing." She gestured to the nightie. "It looked promising on the rack, I swear." She smiled. Sweet, for once.

I picked my jeans up off the floor.

21.

"And now he's being a complete dick."

Evie and I, in my car. We were meeting the Bishops at Squire at six for Coke floats and snacks. I silently prayed that Adina would behave. That Evie and Fred would get along. That we'd all love one another and love our hamburgers and love the diner décor.

"Hello?" Evie leaned forward and knocked on my head. "Are you listening?"

"Yeah. *Yes.*" I swatted her hand away, refocusing. "He's being a dick." I shifted gears. "But wait, why?"

"I don't know. I really don't. He's being bitchy, like—like a *girl.*" Ben. "Supersensitive and weird, and when I ask him what's wrong he says nothing and tells me I'm crazy. But we haven't hung out since Sunday. I mean, I saw him yesterday between calc and chem lab, but he's not returning my texts." She checked her phone.

"Eves."

She looked at me quickly, her eyes shining. "I know, what the fuck, right?" She laughed a little. Two tears rolled down her cheek. "Fuck." She wiped her face, then reached around to the backseat and grabbed her purse.

"You okay?"

"Yeah." She pulled a small plastic container from her bag.

"What's that?"

"Pill box." She lifted the lid and dug out a tiny tablet. "Xanax. Want half?"

"Where'd you get that? You take Xanax?"

She split the pill in two. "Judith. And no, not normally, but I'm having a pretty shitty week." She swallowed half, dry, and offered me the rest.

"Thanks, I'm okay."

"You're sure?"

"Yeah."

"This stuff is amazing. One minute you're a psycho mess, the next? Worry free. Nice, right?"

"Sounds it."

She dumped the pill box back in her bag. "Who are we meeting again?"

"The Bishops."

"Who?

"My *friends*," I said, for the umpteenth time. "You'll see."

"Friends," she echoed softly. "You've never had any other friends."

"I have."

"Barely." She watched out the window. "It's always just been just you and me."

Fries and ranch, four Coke floats, a grilled cheese on rye, and one cherries jubilee.

"I know nothing about you two," Evie said, taking a bite of greasy grilled cheese and shoving the other half my way.

"Really?" Adina's eyes flickered. "We've heard tons about you."

Evie looked at me. "Oh yeah?"

"Yeah," she continued. "Katonah says you two fight like crazy." She picked at a congealed cherry and winked.

"I didn't say that."

Evie swallowed, cocking her head.

"What I said was—" My stomach knotted. "That we were like family. And that, like *family*—" I glared at Adina. "We fight sometimes."

Evie shrugged, taking another bite. "Sounds about right."

I relaxed and sat back. Fred and I exchanged smiles. "You're not eating," I said to him.

He picked up a french fry and wagged it around. "Yum."

I grinned.

"Okay, so, back to you." Evie faced Adina. "You're twins."

"Right."

"So, what can you do?"

"What do you mean?"

"Well, can you, like, read each other's minds?"

"Oh." Adina laughed. "Yeah, absolutely."

"And can you, like, feel each other's pain?"

"Mm, totally," said Fred.

"Fascinating." Evie smiled, leaned forward, and yanked on Fred's scarf. "I like this," she said, softly. "What is this?"

"Cashmere," he said, his face flushing pink.

My head got hot. What the hell was happening? Were they flirting? "Evie's madly in love," I blurted. Her smile vanished.

"Boyfriend?" asked Adina.

"Yeah." She nodded. "But I mean, we're casual."

"Since when?"

She ignored me, facing Fred. "Girlfriend?"

"No."

"Crushes?"

"Can we talk about something else?" I pushed my plate away.

"Why?"

"I don't know."

"Boys are gross, right, Al?"

I shot Evie a look.

"She's cute, right?"

"Stop."

"Just so clean and pristine . . ."

"Evie, shut *up*."

"Hey, Katonah," Fred said. "She's teasing."

"I'm serious!" Evie laughed. "No joke, Alex is like, the perfect virgin."

"*Evie!*" I shrieked.

"What? What's your problem?" She draped an arm over my shoulder. "She's a sensitive soul . . ." Evie cooed. Then: "Seriously, Alex, be happy. Boys love virgins." She took a sloppy bite of Adina's dessert.

After dinner, on the walk to our cars, Adina grabbed my hand.

"Hi," she said.

"Hello."

"You okay?"

Evie and Fred walked ahead.

"I'm fine." Though really, I wasn't.

"How long is she here for?"

"Evie? Just till tomorrow." I pulled my parka tight to my body.

"Must be sad, seeing her go."

"I guess." I glanced up.

"So what's the deal with her and her boyfriend?"

"Ben?"

"Is it serious?"

"Apparently not." Evie was hyper, happy—she let out a shrill squeal and hopped on Fred's back. "She likes boys," I said.

"Clearly."

My eyes watered from the wind.

"It's cold, yeah?"

I nodded.

"Here, come'ere," Adina said, pulling me close. "I'll keep you warm."

22.

Monday morning before school, I crept into bed with my mother.

"Mommy?"

"Hmm?"

Evie was gone. We'd made it through our weekend fight free, but now I was miserable.

"Baby?"

So sad. Eat-a-shitload-of-cookies-and-sleep-for-a-week sad.

"I cooked." Four fried eggs. Two English muffins. Jam. Butter. Green Earl Grey. "Eat with me?" I jerked the tray off the bedside table and set it between us.

"Want some covers?" Mom peeled back the duvet and gestured for me to come closer. I kicked off my sneakers and tugged the blanket over my jeans and sweater. "It's good, babe." She was eating a piece of toast and smiling.

"It's nothing."

"Special occasion?"

Pity party? I cut my egg in half and shrugged.

"Got anything exciting on the agenda today?"

"Nope."

"You?"

"Uh-uh."

"You and Eves have fun this weekend?"

I shoveled some egg into my mouth. "I guess."

"You guess?" She unscrewed the top of the jam jar. "What's that supposed to mean?" She touched my cheek. "Babe, you okay?"

"I'm fine," I said quickly. "Chem quiz today." I sank further under the blankets. "I'm not even remotely prepared."

23.

Adina came careening around a corner, clutching books.

"Hey," I shouted, pepping up. I felt a cozy rush remembering Friday night's exchange. "Adina!" She didn't see me—wait, had she seen me? Her eyes shot left, then settled on my face. I waved. No response. I smiled. She kept walking. Was she looking past me? I turned, looked back, she was gone.

Then: "Guess who?" Something was mauling me.

Fred. "What do you want?" I asked, wriggling free.

"What do you mean, *what do I want*? You okay?" He ruffled my hair and gave me a slight shove. "You look funny."

"Thanks." I kept on toward chem, feeling supremely let down. He seemed so different now. Less mine, more Evie's. "Your sister just iced me."

"Adina?"

"No, your other sister."

He laughed. I didn't. "Hey. Hey, Katonah."

"What?"

"Did I do something wrong?"

Wrong? No. Fred didn't belong to me. He didn't belong to anyone (besides Adina, maybe, and she'd waved the warning flag weeks ago while I'd laughed and looked the other way). "Sorry," I said. "It's not you; it's me."

"Now there's a line I love."

"No, I mean—I'm in a mood."

"Why?"

You <3 Evie. You want to kiss her and hold her and take off her clothes. "I—chem quiz." I waved around my index cards.

"Oh. Well, break a leg."

"Thanks." I started back toward class.

"Hey, Katonah—after school. You have plans?"

I didn't reply. I felt a sudden swell of hope, then beat it backward.

"Let's drive somewhere."

I eyed Fred warily.

"You don't like driving?"

"Yeah, I do. Of course I do."

"So, come with," he said softly. "I feel like getting away," he said. His lashes fluttered rhythmically: *Quick, slow, quick.*

* * *

We drove. Past Grams's, past Fred's, over the Meadow Marsh town line. We saw woods. Brown fields. A horse. A liquor store. "Where are we going?"

"I dunno." He changed the track on the stereo. "You wanna go back?"

"No." It was getting dark. We'd been in the car for forty-five minutes and hadn't really talked much. "Where's Adina?"

He rolled down the windows and switched on the heat. "Piano."

"Really?" I couldn't picture it. I looked at Fred. My hair blew forward.

"What?" said Fred. "What're you looking at?"

Him, I was looking at *him*. The outline of his skinny bod, the slope of his nose, his kinky hair, and huge feet. "I don't know. *You*, I guess. You look different driving."

"How so?"

"Adult, sort of. I don't know, I can't explain it."

He glanced over. "You're funny right now."

"I am?" I felt high. A little wired. I babbled on: "You do this a lot?"

"What?"

"Take drives."

"I guess."

"With Adina?"

He shook his head. "She gets antsy in the car."

I leaned against the headrest. "Then who with?" *Other girls other girls other girls?* "Other girls?"

He laughed—

"What?"

—then looked at me quizzically. "Other girls? Have you ever seen me with anyone besides Adina?"

I hadn't, and really, what would it matter anyway? Adina—*Evie*, even—now seemed so very far away. "I'm a girl," I said.

He took a beat. "Yes, you are."

I'm a girl. It suddenly clicked. I was a *girl*, not a virgin, a baby, a prude. "So why do I get to come along?" I asked, feeling momentarily bold.

"You're fishing."

"For *what*?"

He laughed and looked over. "I'm happy you're here, Katonah."

Fred dropped me home a little after seven. We'd driven sixty-five miles out and back.

"Thanks."

"What for?" I undid my seatbelt.

"For coming." He shifted the car into neutral and took his foot off the clutch. "You know, with your mood earlier." *Right. My mood.* "So." He shrugged. "I'm just glad you came."

"Yeah."

He was looking at me. I let him look. "So," he said again, leaning across my seat and popping the lock on the door. "See you later?" He lingered. The way boys in movies sometimes do. For a split second I considered tilting forward, pushing into him. *I'd like to feel wanted,* I thought. Instead I kept perfectly still. Fred pulled back.

"All right," I said, annoyed with myself. Evie would have done something. She would have made something *significant* happen. I collected my bag and books. "See you tomorrow," I said, shoving the door wide open.

Inside, Mom was steaming rice for stir-fry. *Progress!* I dropped my keys, coat, and bag by the door.

"Babe."

"Hi." I stole a tomato from the salad bowl.

"You hungry?"

"Always."

She seemed chipper. *Sane.* Then I noticed the tall tumbler she was clutching. "Kool Aid?" Transparent pink.

"Just a touch of rosé."

My mood sank.

"Where were you?" she asked, sipping gingerly, redirecting the conversation.

"Driving."

"Your car's out front."

"No, I know. I was with Fred." I took another tomato slice

and nibbled morosely. "We dropped my car back here after school."

Mom's brow lifted. "The boy."

I rolled my eyes. "He's not *The Boy*. He's my friend."

She put down her glass and my stomach unclenched. "Invite him over. His sister, too—what's her name?"

"Adina."

She giggled. "What kind of a name is Adina?"

"A rich one."

"Well," she said, picking a clean cucumber from the sink, "invite them. Some night next week? I'll cook."

I looked down at the checkered linoleum flooring. "I mean, they're pretty busy most days. . . ." I didn't want her making dinner for the Bishops. She'd drink too much, cry, and wreck everything.

"How busy can they be?" She snacked on a cuc. "You're together day and night, right?"

I nodded, refusing to look up. I was a terrible daughter, I knew it, but shame—shame trumps guilt.

"Just ask, all right?" She tickled my chin.

I nodded, but I wouldn't, *couldn't,* ask.

"I'll make my stuffed shells."

24.

Morning. Switching out books for the following block.

"Katonah."

I peeked past my locker door and there stood Adina. Smiling, skinny, all decked in black.

"Hi." *Friends again?* "How's your morning?"

"Late for lab, what else is new?" I pulled my chem book free from a tall stack of crap, and down fell Fred's caramels. "Shit!" I squealed, lunging for them. "Gah." I'd missed. I bent down and scooped them up off the industrial carpeting. "Chocolate?" I offered, unfolding the small paper bag and tipping it toward Adina.

"Caramels!" Her face lit up. "Are these from Dusty's? They're dark, right?"

"Yeah, they're dark. They're incredible." I handed her the bag and slammed my door shut. "They're from Fred. Take some."

She glanced up. "From Fred, really?"

"Yeah." I zipped my tote and stood. "Have some. Which way are you headed?"

Her smiled died. "I'm—nowhere, I'm free this block."

"Walk with me?"

She followed along, suddenly sullen. "So. Fred got you caramels."

"Sweet, right?"

"Very." She linked an arm through mine, yanking me close. "I heard you two went for a drive yesterday."

"We did."

"How was that?"

"Really nice." She was clutching my arm so tight it was tingling.

"That's great, you know. You're friends, that's nice." She was squinting and staring and clucking her tongue. "I'm confused, though."

"Why? What about?"

"Well, about Fred."

"What about him?"

"About you and Fred. You know, dating."

"But we're not."

"Right, no, I know, it's just—he's giving you things. You're going for drives."

"So?"

"So, you know how he can be."

"Right." I eyed her sideways. "All those girls . . ."

"I'm just trying to help," she continued, dodging my wary glare. "I mean, you saw him the other night with your friend." My heart dropped. "I'm watching out for you."

Now we were face to face, hovering outside my chem class.

"Well, thanks," I said. "For your help."

"Yeah." She passed back my chocolates.

"You don't want any?" I asked, rolling the bag shut.

"I shouldn't." She patted her concave belly. "You, though, eat up. You're way curvier—you can carry the extra pounds."

25.

Lunch. Charlotte and Libby noshed on tuna sandwiches and PB&Js.

"Why aren't you eating?"

Curvier. Curvaceous. What was that, anyway? Adina code for fat? "Huge breakfast," I lied, crumpling Fred's caramels into a small ball and shoving them into my bag.

"Sounds nourishing."

"Absolutely." I was hungry now, and irritable.

"Where are the Bishops?"

"Last lunch." I poked my gut with my pinky.

"Any good gossip?" Libby's mouth was full of pickles and white bread and canned fish.

"Like?"

"How's your boyfriend?" Charlotte asked.

"I don't have a boyfriend."

"Sorry, your crush."

"Who?" Libby's smile was crooked.

I shot eyeball daggers at Charlotte. "No one." Then: "Can you stop? Please?"

"Fine." She looked around, then down. "How's Liz?"

"Liz?" Libby asked.

"My mother." Then, to Charlotte, "She's fine, thanks for asking."

"My mom said she wasn't doing too great."

I resisted the urge to reach out and slap someone. "Well, your mom is wrong. And she's barely been by the house, so how would she know?"

"They talk."

"When?"

"I don't know, they *talk*. On the phone. Are you *always* around?" *No*. In fact, I was *never* around. I suddenly felt like bawling. Charlotte continued, her voice softening. "I only asked to be nice."

I nodded, looking up.

"I like your mom."

"Okay."

Libby put down her sandwich and Charlotte's face got all squishy. "I'm sorry about your dad, Alex."

I tilted my face forward and two tears shot onto my lap, staining my jeans a darker blue. "Thanks." I was mortified. "Can we stop talking about this now?"

Libby passed me a crumpled napkin. I dabbed my eyes, then fanned my hands in front of my face. "It's fine. I'm fine, see? I'm just hungry."

"I thought you said you'd eaten."

"I—I did," I stuttered at Libby. "I ate a ton, I did, but I'm hungry again."

"That happens to me too," she offered. "I'm bottomless, I swear it." She smiled. "Want some sandwich?"

"Maybe," I said, sniffling, drying my cheeks. "Just a bite."

26.

"You're avoiding me."

"I'm not," I said. I was wearing Grams's pink padded housecoat and lying on the floor in the den.

"Seriously, you are," Evie maintained. "I've called twice since Sunday."

I clutched the phone.

"So?"

What to say? *I'm pissed at you for flirting with a boy who's not my boyfriend?* "How's Ben?"

"Great. *So* great. He flipped when he realized I'd spent the entire weekend with you. He's been like, psychotically clingy since Monday." She was chewing something. "You sure you're not mad?"

The TV murmured gameshow noises.

"Evie?"

"Hmm?"

I'm a girl, I thought. *A real girl just like you.* I could like a boy, stake my claim, kiss whomever. I didn't *have* to be *me* forever. *Prim. Good.* "Can I—I want to ask you something."

"Okay."

I sucked in a whole bunch of air. "Why—" I asked, my voice sounding shaky and thin. "Why, if you're so into Ben, if you love Ben so much . . . ," Was I really going to ask this? I clutched some rug, bracing myself. ". . . do you flirt with other boys?"

The chewing stopped. "What do you mean? Like who?"

I took another breath. "Like, Fred, for example. Why flirt with Fred?"

I expected attitude, a bitchy retort, but, "Do you like him?" is what she said instead.

"I dunno," I said, softly. "I might."

"Oh." A beat. "Oh, Al."

"It's fine."

"No, Al—"

"It's okay." I exhaled. "I'm not trying to make you feel bad."

"No, I know, but, had I known—"

"What?"

"Had I known, I wouldn't have—" She stopped. "Al, you never like *anyone.*"

"So?"

"So I just assumed—"

"What? That I'd never like anyone, *ever*? That my entire life I'd just exist in some chaste little bubble?" I pinched some back fat.

"No."

"So, *what*? It's just so impossible for you to imagine that someone might actually like me back?"

"Alex."

"What?" My eyes stung. I muted the television.

"I'm sorry," she said. "I just—that thing with Fred—that's what I do. I feel bad about one guy and find another. If I'd've known . . . Al, you never like anyone."

"You said that already."

"No, I mean—this is like, a big deal."

"It's not."

"It *is*. You know it is." She paused for a second. "Have you told him how you feel?"

"I can't tell him that."

"Why not?"

"Why not?" I repeated, "Why not? Because. It's humiliating."

"Hold on, okay?" There was quiet, followed by some loud crunching.

"What're you eating?"

"Sorry. Sorry, I'm starving. Chips. Cheese sandwich."

My stomach gurgled.

"So telling him—" She continued, mouth full, "I don't get it—what have you got to lose?"

"Um, my dignity?"

"Your dignity? How can dignity be lost?"

"Are you kidding me?" How could she *not* understand? "Liking someone—*so* embarrassing."

"You're crazy."

"I'm not."

"How is liking someone embarrassing?"

Why was this so hard to grasp? "What if that person doesn't like you back?"

"So?"

"So that's *humiliating.*"

"*How*? You're honest, you put yourself out there . . . Take a risk, Katonah. Isn't that what they call you?"

"It is."

"Well?"

"Well what?" I wasn't ready to risk anything.

Evie took another crunchy bite. "Sorry I came on to your boyfriend."

"He's *not* my boyfriend."

"Jesus, Al," she said. "Lighten up."

27.

It was official. I liked Fred.

"Remote, please?"

We were at their place, always. Never mine. Mom was still pushing: "Shells and cheese, your twins! Invite them here, babe." But I couldn't.

"Catch." Fred tossed Adina the remote. We'd been drinking wine spritzers and watching shitty TV all afternoon.

"Thanks." She pointed it like a pistol, flipping quickly through channels. "What the hell? Why is everything court programming and news?"

I wasn't drunk enough.

"Because it's four thirty," said Fred, sitting up. "Nothing's on at four thirty." He leaned forward, carelessly brushing my thigh with his hand. I jumped. "Katonah, hey. You okay?"

"Hmm?" I looked away from the TV. I must have looked

insane, since "Jesus, what's wrong with you?" is what Fred said next.

"Why? What do you mean?" I touched my face.

"You look scared." He laughed. "Something I said?"

I smiled and sank back. "I'm fine."

"More spritzer?" He picked up the pitcher.

"Thanks." I nodded.

"Summer drinks on winter days . . ." Adina stood up. "This sucks." She chucked the changer. "I'm getting a movie. Any requests?"

"Nothing Holocaust-y," said Fred.

"Har, har." She skipped toward the steps.

Fred turned to me. "You sure you're okay?"

"I'm fine." Adina was gone. "You drunk?"

He shook his head. "Weak drinks," he said, shifting sideways. Then, quietly: "Is it Adina?"

"Is *what* Adina?"

"You just—you seem upset."

"I told you, I'm not." I was irritable and behaving crazy. Someone was lying to me. But really, did I care?

"I mean . . ." He propped himself up on both elbows. "Did she say something to you?"

Where to start? "Why'd you break up with that girl?"

"Audrey?"

Adina's heels smacked the wide wooden staircase.

"Your call—black, white, and boring? Or creepy modern

romance?" She walked forward, holding two DVD cases. "Brother, pick a hand."

"Ah." Fred looked from me to her. "That one," he said, pointing left.

She shot an arm up in victory—"Creepy modern romance!"—and threw down onto the couch, wedging herself between me and Fred. "Fantastic choice. So . . ." She took a sip of spritzer. "What did I miss?"

"Not much."

"Should I put the movie in?"

"Sure."

She got back up. "Shit," she said, grabbing her head. "I'm hammered."

"That's because you weigh, like, two pounds," said Fred.

She smiled smugly, crouched in front of the television, and popped the DVD into the player. "This is fun, isn't it?" She twisted around. "Us three? Together?"

"It is," said Fred, glancing over. "Katonah?"

"Hmm?

"You having fun?"

"Oh, absolutely," I insisted, clutching a throw pillow to my chest, wishing it was just us, me and him, *alone, alone, alone*. . . . "Wine spritzers and movies. What could be better?"

28.

"Cute skates."

I blinked at Ben. "They're rentals."

We—Evie, me, Ben—sat on bleachers at the Katonah indoor ice rink picking baby marshmallows out of vending-machine cocoa.

"Well, they look good on you."

They're SKATES. How good can they look?

Evie downed the last of her drink and stood, wobbling. "Are we gonna do this or what?"

Skating was Ben's idea. He was a pro. "Fine, I'm just—I'm not that good." I'd taken one lesson as a kid and quit.

"Gimme your hand," said Evie.

I did. Together we teetered toward the rink, stepped onto slick ice. "Fun, right?"

No. I was on a date with my best friend and her boyfriend.

Ben yanked Evie close, tugging me along too. They kissed. He upped his pace. "Hey. Hey, guys? Slow down, please?" I dragged pathetically behind. "Guys?"

"Oh, come on, Alex, you're doing great."

"I'm not, actually." I let go of Evie's hand, grasping for the rink railing.

"Alex," she called, frowning, waving. "Hey!" She skidded to a stop. "Come here."

"I can't."

"Come. Here." She gestured frantically with one hand.

I slid forward, slowly, leaning inward on my ankles.

"There," she said, taking my hand again. "We'll let Ben skate on his own."

"Sorry."

"It's fine," she said, waving a weak good-bye to her boyfriend. "I'd rather skate with you." We locked arms. "So."

"So."

"How's home?"

H-o-m-e. That word sounded so peculiar. "Which one?"

"*Here*, home."

Was here still home? "Fine, I guess."

"How's your dad?"

"Still slutty."

Evie gripped me tighter. "Any new news?"

"Like?"

"Oh, come on." She pressed her nose to my nose.

"I know what you want—" *Fred.* "And I didn't—nothing's happening."

"Well have you seen him?"

"Yeah. I mean, I see him a lot."

"Well have you said anything?"

"*No.* I told you, I'm not like you. I can't just make . . . big declarations."

"Well, okay, you don't have to actually declare *anything*"—she turned, skating backward—"but you might, like, I don't know, kiss him?"

"No way."

"*Actions*, Al."

I rolled my eyes.

"God," she said, and swung around so she was facing forward again. "You're incorrigible."

I laughed. "That's a big word, Eves."

"Yeah, and there's more where that came from." She slapped my arm, hard.

29.

Squash, apples, pecans, honey—Fred and I were back from the store with bags of lumpy produce.

"Hello?!"

"Kitchen!" screamed Adina. "Bring me my things!" She was making a sweet squash casserole for dinner.

"Here." We unloaded onto the floor, emptying our canvas totes. "Create!" yelled Fred, pounding the granite countertop with both fists. Adina grabbed a massive knife and gave us both once-overs.

"You're wearing Fred's sweater."

"Oh." I looked at Fred. "Yeah, it got cold."

"Cute," she said, jamming the knife tip into the head of the squash. "You two look like a couple." I felt my face flush, then quietly gripped the edges of Fred's cream wool cardigan. "Katonah, you're blushing."

"I'm hot."

"I thought you said you were cold." She leaned into the knife and the squash broke in two.

"Hey," Fred said to Adina. "You need our help or no?"

"Go play," she said lightly, dragging a baking sheet out from under the stovetop. "You've done plenty already." She curtsied and pulled a bottle of red from the wine rack.

By dinner, she was completely blitzed.

"Why don't you sit down and eat something," suggested Fred. He and I were eating on a checkerboard blanket in the den while Adina danced around gripping a tall glass of Bordeaux. I'd taken off Fred's sweater.

"Adina."

She put down her glass and did one perfect, pretty pirouette. "What?" Her skirt billowed. "What's wrong? You don't like my squash?"

"It's terrific," Fred said, extending a hand. "Come sit."

She bounced forward, collapsing with a flourish.

"Here." He piled some squash onto his fork. "Eat this," he said, feeding his sister.

She chewed, sitting back. "Pretty good."

"You're a wiz in the kitchen."

"*And* on the dance floor."

"Here," he said, fixing Adina a small plate.

"I can't eat all that." The squash serving was smaller than my fist.

"You can."

She took the plate, inspecting. "You're sure?"

"Absolutely."

She took three or four small, measured bites.

Fred whispered, "The trick is"—he smelled like wood smoke and candied nuts—"she'll eat if she's liquored up."

I took another spoonful and looked down at my thighs. I had, easily, twenty-five pounds on Adina.

"You good? You want more?"

I set down my plate. "No, I'm stuffed."

He pushed into me. "You sure?"

Adina let out a heavy sigh. She patted her face with a paper towel, glancing up. "You two."

"What?"

"God, look at you both." She wagged a finger. "Do you have to be so obvious about it?" She sipped some wine, then set down her glass. "Look," she said, batting her lashes at me. "You know what he wants to do to you?"

"Adina," Fred snapped. His voice was hard and low.

"Do you?" She was on hands and knees now. "You want me to show you?"

I froze. Fred froze. No one moved but Adina, who was leaning forward now, her lips parting. She pressed her mouth to my mouth. Her tongue touched my teeth and I jumped back, rattled. "Hey."

For a second, no one said anything. Some French lady sang on the stereo.

"Jesus," Fred spat. "What the fuck is wrong with you?"

Adina laughed.

Fred picked me up by my elbow. "You okay?"

I felt zilch. Nothing but shiny numbness.

"You want me to take you home?"

"I—that's fine." I wasn't entirely sure what had just happened.

Adina stayed on the ground, slumped over, giggling.

"Come on," said Fred, picking my purse and coat off the ground and dragging me toward the door. "We're leaving."

The first few minutes in the car neither of us really said much. Fred shifted around a bit—a little left, a little right—then came out with this: "I'm sorry."

"For what?" I rolled my window down a crack. He had the heat cranked high. I was suffocating. "She's drunk, it's okay."

"She just—" A bolt of paranoia struck. How had I gotten here? Who was this guy? "She can be funny sometimes." The car stopped. "She tries to make people feel bad?" He said it like a question. Then: "Are you completely freaked out?" We were moving again. Toward Grams's house, a few yards off.

"I don't know. No?" I wasn't sure. Adina's kiss hadn't felt

any different than Evie's practice kisses: soft and inconsequential. But her highs and lows, her I'm-your-friend-wait-no-I'm-not shtick left me feeling way less stellar. "Thanks," I added, undoing my seat belt. "For the lift." We were home.

"Yeah. Thanks for being so cool about this."

"That's me," I said, gripping the door handle. "Cool as a cuc."

"A what?"

"Cucumber. It's an expression."

We watched each other for a bit. Fred had two small drops of something red—wine, maybe—splattered across the sleeve of his sweater. I had the shameful urge to touch my tongue to it.

"From, like, 1952?"

"Exactly." I had no energy to muster a grin. "I'm so old school," I said, and got out of the car.

30.

Morning was warm. High fifties and girls were in tank tops and light cardigans. I walked to class with my parka tucked under one arm and a hot tea in my other hand. I had my eyes peeled for Fred. I hadn't seen him or Adina since the night before and it was already third block.

"Dyke," sneezed some douchy football guy from my French section. I looked around to see what poor soul he was gay-bashing that day, then noticed a pile of brunettes in field hockey skirts gazing in my direction. I checked over my shoulder and saw Libby and Charlotte huddled against their lockers, watching me. They were sharing a tube of Pringles.

"Hi," I said to Charlotte, sidestepping through the crowd. "What's with the look?"

"What look?"

"Oh come on, you guys were staring." I swung back around and noticed two guys from chem class giggling like toddlers. "Seriously? *What* is so goddamn funny?" Libby looked at the ground. Charlotte popped the top back on her chips. "Anyone?"

"No big deal."

"What?"

"Nothing."

"Oh come on, it's obviously not nothing."

Charlotte licked her lips. "We heard."

"What about?"

"You know. Last night." She sniffed.

I felt dazed and disconnected. "What about last night?" What could they possibly know?

"You kissed Adina," Charlotte said. "I thought you liked boys."

I pulled back, startled. "I do." They looked at me blankly. "I'm sorry, what exactly did you hear?"

They glanced at each other. "That you kissed Adina. That you, like, wanted to be with her, but she wasn't into it."

"Who did you hear that from?"

Libby snuck a thin lock of hair between her teeth and chewed.

"Adina."

"She wouldn't say that."

"That's exactly what she said."

"You heard that from her?"

"I mean, I overheard her telling Glen Kelly."

My head got cold. "You heard wrong."

"I didn't."

Why would she say that? Why twist what's true?

"Alex?"

I turned on tiptoe.

"It doesn't matter to us. Whether you like girls or not. We don't care."

"Gee, Charlotte, thanks." I walked on.

I waited for Adina outside her last class. I waited and watched while a crowd of kids sped by, pushing toward their lockers and cars.

"Adina." She was only a few feet away. I reached out and grabbed her arm. "Hey."

"Oh." She kept walking. "I'm rushing, what's up?"

"Well—" I was jogging alongside. "I wanted to ask you something."

"So ask."

"Can you stop moving, please?" I tugged on her sleeve. "For like, two seconds?"

"I'm late."

"For what?"

"Piano."

"Adina."

"*What*?" She stopped. Her lips were pursed. "Quickly, okay? I have to go."

"Did you . . . ?" is how I started. I didn't want to have to say it. "What are you telling people?"

"About?" She feigned oblivion. "Can't this wait?"

"Not really."

"So? Spit it out."

What was she? Friend? Foe? "Did you tell people about that kiss?"

Real quick: "No."

"You didn't? Because people are saying you did."

Without pause: "I didn't say shit." Her cheeks were pink. "Clearly *you* said something. Or Fred."

"Why would *I* say something?"

"Who knows? Maybe you've got some creepy crush on me and this is your way of expressing it."

I flinched. "Hey. I'm not a liar."

"Oh, and you think I am?" She smiled, and started off.

"Adina," I called, wringing my hands, ready to cry.

"I'm late." She flicked her wrist—one cruel little wave. "Gotta go."

31.

I lay on a towel in Grams's backyard; grass below, sky up high. I felt fine there. Crisp breeze. Late-day light. My own meditative retreat.

"You sleeping?"

Or not. It was Fred. I sat up. "You're here?"

He kneeled down next to me. "Yeah, me."

I made room on the towel. "Did you hear the news?"

"What news?"

"About me and Adina?"

He blinked.

"You didn't hear?"

"What?"

"We kissed last night. You remember. *I* kissed her. I told her I liked girls and that I really wanted to be with her, but, you know, Adina, she's straight, so I got shut down."

I picked at a cuticle. "It's all over school."

"Oh."

"*Oh?* That's all?" He wouldn't meet my eyes. He looked weak, which enraged me. "What's wrong with you?" No response. I took a breath, then came out with this: "Why does she *hate* me so much?"

"It's not—she doesn't hate you."

"Why would she lie? I don't even care, you know? I don't care if people think I'm something I'm not. I have two real friends here—or, okay, *one* friend, I guess. *You.*" I hooked my hands underneath my knees. "Or, I dunno, are you even my friend?"

"Hey." He touched my shoulder. "Of course I am."

"So?"

He took a tiny breath, "This is about me," he said, and picked a few blades of new grass. "She doesn't like people."

"Yeah, you say that a lot."

"She gets jealous."

"Of what?"

"Other girls." He dug his nail into the dirt, tracing a deep, jagged line.

"She's your sister."

"Yeah, I know." He shook his head. "You think we're weird."

"I just—I don't get it. She *controls* your life."

"She doesn't."

"She *does*. She doesn't let you have friends."

He put his hand near my hand. "Yeah, well, you freak her out."

"Yeah? *Why*?" I was livid. "I'm a mouse. I'm a field mouse and she's a fucking piranha."

He laughed.

"Don't laugh." I whacked his arm.

He caught my hand and held it. "I'm sorry," he said. His smile fell. "I like you. She *knows* I like you." He laced his fingers through my fingers.

"You like me?" I asked.

Then I kissed him.

I pressed my lips to his lips, moving as close to him as I could possibly get. I rubbed my fingers against his blazer lapel and pulled him closer by a belt loop with my free hand. He kissed back, touching my shoulders, my hair, opening his mouth and pushing his tongue against my tongue. Sliding his pointer finger lightly past my ear, curling it around and down the front of my neck and stopping at the dip in the V of my sweater.

"Alex." He pulled back.

"What's wrong?" I asked, breathless and a little dizzy.

"I'm sorry," he said, getting up on one knee.

"For what?"

"I should go."

"Wait, why?"

He was standing now. I was still on the ground.

"I'm really sorry. It's late."

"It's four thirty." My eyes burned.

"Tomorrow," he said, backing away real quick. "I'll see you then?"

What had I done? Where was he going? "I—okay."

He waved limply, then he was gone. I wiped my wet cheeks with dirty fingertips.

32.

I went to Dad's. I didn't call ahead, I just showed up. Quarter to nine, Thursday night. I wiggled my key in the back door lock, letting myself in. "Hello?"

He was on the couch, TV blaring, an arm draped around slutty Caroline. "Al?"

I dropped my bag and Chicken came running. She jumped, pawing my shoulders and chest.

"Al."

Caroline leaped to her feet, adjusting the straps on her tank top. She was braless. "Alex."

I felt nauseated. Sick seeing them together, so cozy. "It's me," I said, hovering by the door with the dog. "I should've called, sorry."

"What're you doing here?" Dad asked, muting the TV and getting up. "You've got school tomorrow, yeah?"

He walked toward the back entryway where I stood.

"Yeah, I just—needed to get away for a bit."

He leaned in for a kiss and I stepped sideways, pushing past him toward the den. "What's all this?" Stacks of brown boxes with liquor logos lined the walls along the hall. "You going somewhere?"

Caroline stood nervously by the coat rack covering her boobs with her forearms. "We weren't expecting you."

"We?" I said, beelining for a stack and peeling back a box lid. "Is this my leftover stuff? Why are you moving it?"

"It's not yours, babe."

I spun on both heels, thrown. "Well whose is it?" Dad slipped an arm around Caroline's waist. "Oh." My throat knotted. "Oh, it's yours?" My voice broke. "What, you're, like, living here now?"

Neither said yes. Dad skipped yes and went straight to: "We were going to tell you."

We again. "When?"

"I've only been here a couple of weeks."

"Weeks?" I looked at Dad. "You're not even divorced yet. Is that legal?" Back to Caroline. "How old are you, anyways?"

"Alex."

I dashed passed them, grabbing my bag. "I'm going upstairs," I said, too tired to drive back to Grams's. "I'll leave first thing, okay?"

"Al, you can stay as long as you like." Then again, "*Al.*"

"What?" I considered blurting it, telling Caroline about the porch incident between Dad and Mom, the kissing. "It's fine," I said, resisting. It seemed like a shitty move—*outing* Dad to his baby girlfriend. Besides, at this point I had zero hope for parental reconciliation. "I'm going upstairs," I said, my mind jumping to Fred. "I'll be out of your hair by morning." I pounded the steps, leaving Caroline and Dad in the dust.

I slept in, got up at eleven, and went downstairs in my socks and T-shirt. Caroline was on the floor unpacking books and broken CDs.

"Don't you work?" I asked, breezing past her toward the kitchen.

"Funny."

"I'm not kidding," I said, grabbing the kettle off the stove and filling it with tap water. "Aren't you a secretary or something?"

"Or something," she said softly. So soft I could barely hear. Then: "I'm between jobs."

"Oh." I switched on the gas and shuffled forward.

"Don't you have school?" she asked, not looking up. She was inspecting the spine of a paperback.

"I'm not going," I said, resting against the doorframe, watching her. Wondering what she saw in Dad. What he saw in *her*—that was clear.

"You want food?"

"I'm leaving."

"When? Your dad'll be back by one."

"I'll be gone," I said, following the call of the kettle.

"You should stay."

"That's okay."

"I mean you're here, it's the weekend. What's one more day?"

I filled my cup with steaming water. "Three's a crowd. . . ." I mumbled, dropping a green tea bag into my mug. *Three. Three* used to feel right. Me, Mom, Dad—the perfect unit. Now *three* felt lopsided and odd. Me, Evie, Ben. Me, Adina, Fred. Someone was always, *always* getting pushed to the side. "Why?" I asked Caroline. "Why do you want me to stay?"

She glanced up. Her eyes, pretty and blank and blue. "You make your dad happy."

I thought about Mom, home alone in pieces. Dad had Caroline. Mom had me, and I was *here*.

"Stay for lunch at least?"

I needed to leave. "Can't. Besides, I can afford to skip a meal," I muttered, shuffling past and back upstairs. "I'm fat enough as is," I said, slamming my bedroom door shut.

33.

I spent the remainder of my weekend home with Mom, watching her smile wanly while wondering whether it was worth it to confess what I knew about Dad and Caroline. Fred hadn't called once. Not even to ask why I'd missed school Friday. Clearly I'd wrecked everything. I'd taken a perfectly good friendship and made it all creepy and weird. If I'd been Evie, that kiss would have led to something sexy and momentous. But I was babyish and unappealing. *Fine,* I thought, alone in bed Sunday night. *You don't want me? Lesson learned.*

Monday, I ate lunch alone on the field hockey field. Baby carrots and warm Diet Coke. Then, feeling hollow and nauseated, I walked to class. I passed the twins on my way. Fred's eyes flicked in my direction, and my legs shook. Adina moved past without the teensiest glance.

* * *

At home, I sat with Mom on the couch downstairs. She lay on her side, her feet in my lap, laughing at some shitty rerun on channel four. Do I tell her? Keep quiet? The last thing I wanted was her feeling hopeless and miserable again—already she'd been knocked sideways and down.

"You want soda?" I patted her ankles then stood.

"Hmm?"

"I'm getting a Coke. You want something?"

She sat up, curling her knees to her chest. "Thanks for the foot rub, babe."

"Yeah."

"Grab me a water?"

I moved to the kitchen, the TV lighting my way. I pulled a Coke and a water bottle off the fridge door, then mustered the nerve to say, "Mommy?" I would come clean about Caroline's move. She'd hear it from me, not Dad—perhaps that would soften the blow?

"Babe?" A muffled *ding ding ding*. "Babe, your phone." I ran back to the den, dropped the drinks on the sofa, and grabbed my cell off the coffee table. One new text. From Fred. My heart sped up.

"Who is it?"

"Charlotte Kincaid." An easy lie. Why burden her with shitty drama?

I'm sorry, it said. *Can I see you?*

I hit reply, then tapped nervously at my keypad. *Sorry. With Mom,* I wrote.

Seconds later: *I'll come to you. Please?*

I glanced at my mother. Sipping her water, clutching a pillow, she looked so small, like a girl. "I want candy," I said, circling the couch. "You want anything from the liquor store?"

"You're going out?"

"I'll be back in twenty minutes."

She looked down at my hands, still clutching the phone.

"Be back soon, okay?" The Dad news could wait. I bent down and kissed her forehead. "You want chocolate?"

"Always."

I grabbed my coat, keys, and lunged for the door.

We met at the 7-Eleven. We sat in the parking lot, in the front seat of my car, not talking. Until: "You're furious."

"No." I spoke quickly. "I'm really not."

He smelled sweet and smoky, like cigarettes and suckers.

"You hate me."

"I don't, no, why would you say that? I'm embarrassed," I said, wiping my nose, looking down. "You embarrassed me."

"How?"

"How?" I let out a small laugh. "You really have to ask?"

We were touching. Two palms. Fingers entwined. "The other day—I didn't mean to freak out."

I shrugged.

"Audrey Glick?" he said. "She made that girl miserable."

"Adina?"

He nodded.

"What happened with her?"

"Nothing happened. She's at Sacred Heart in Brooksville, alive and wearing a kilt." He faced me. He let go of my hand and twisted my wrist toward the ceiling. "She's not a bad person, Alex." He said this softly, tracing a blue vein on my arm *up up up*. "She thinks she's protecting me." His finger lingered at my inner elbow.

"From who?" I got a chill.

"I dunno. You?" He laughed a little. "Absurd, right? The other day—" He stopped. "I just didn't want—" Another pause. "She's a little crazy, okay? Let me talk to her first?"

"First?"

"Let me tell her how I feel?"

Something rattled around in my chest. "How *do* you feel?" I asked, wondering what this was—a confession? Declaration? Did he *love me want me need me*?

"I feel great," he said, leaning back against the windowpane, looking bright. "Right now I just feel—totally great."

34.

After school, Tuesday.

Audrey Glick.

I shot down the candy aisle of CVS, dropping jelly beans, Twizzlers, and mini Twix bars into my shopping basket. I'd been on an Audrey Glick kick all morning: Was she cuter than me? Smarter? Had Fred slept with her? Loved her?

I paid for my crap, popped open a Twix, and wandered outside. It was sunny and cool. I looked left: an antique shop, a tobacconist, a tailor. To my right: the local library branch. I went inside, found an empty computer station at the back of the lab, and Googled "Audrey Glick."

There were hundreds of pages. A gazillion Audrey Glicks. One, a teacher; another, a bioengineer; yet another, a book blogger. I found my Audrey, *Fred's* Audrey, on page eleven: "Audrey Glick . . . Brooksville Sacred Heart . . ." I clicked the link. There was a photo, an action shot—Audrey alongside two other girls in field hockey jerseys and knee socks. All three wielded sticks. She was the one hunched over, working the ball. She was shiny and clean; a sporty brunette. The braid down her back spoke volumes. It said, "I ride horses. I excel academically. Boys love me."

I closed the page and stepped away from the computer. A jealous twinge tickled my gut. I popped open another Twix and shoved the entire thing in my mouth.

I found Mom upstairs, blinds drawn, asleep at four p.m. *What now?* I stepped forward into the dark. Her room smelled like stuck air and sleep. I put one hand on either shoulder and rocked her awake. "Mommy?"

She rolled over.

"You okay?"

"I'm sleeping. What do you need?"

"Nothing, I just—" I let my hands fall from her shoulders. "Are you okay?"

"Fine."

"You're sure?"

She opened one eye. "Was she there? At Dad's?"

"Who?"

"Come on, Alex."

I didn't answer. I watched Mom watch me.

"Let me sleep, please?" She rolled away, toward the wall.

"Mommy—"

"Please, Alex. Go downstairs and let me sleep. There's a frozen lasagna defrosting in the fridge."

"That's fine, I don't want it."

"Alex."

"What?"

She curled one shoulder toward the mattress and pulled the sheet to her chin. "Shut the door, will you?"

I got up.

35.

"Are you ever gonna ask me inside?"

Fred and I were sitting on Grams's porch floor, using a picnic blanket for warmth. It was seven and dark. Mom was upstairs still.

"I told you. You can come over but you can't come in."

"Why?"

"Because."

"Because *why*?" Fred looked glowy in the pink porch light. "I wanna see your room."

"It's not *my* room," I said. "It's the guest room. My room is in Katonah."

"So take me there."

"I can't."

"Why not?"

I stretched my legs long, crossing my ankles. "Because that's not—that's not home either."

He gave me a sympathetic shrug, tugging the blanket up and slipping a hand between my thighs. The gesture was quick and sent a shock through me. I gasped.

"Sorry." He pulled his hand back. "I didn't mean—I meant—I was trying to comfort you, not feel you up."

I put my hand where his hand had been. My leg pulsed. I looked at him.

"Are you really freaked out? You look really freaked out."

I was shaking, only, "No." I wasn't freaked out. Or cold. I felt warm and alert. "You could've left it there," I said.

"What?" His voice sounded small.

I took his hand and put it back were it'd been. I slid closer. So our hips and shoulders lined up. "Like that," I said.

His face flushed.

After a minute: "Adina's sorry," he said. He whispered it.

I wanted so badly to believe. Adina had given us her blessing and now Fred could love me freely and wouldn't life be stellar, everyone loving everyone else?

"She's making Peruvian tomorrow. Come?"

So much of me touching so much of Fred. "Peruvian, huh?"

"I want you there." He was like my own personal space heater. "We both just—really want to make things right." Then: "She's not a monster, Katonah."

"You're sure?"

He yanked his hand away, stung.

"No," I said, grabbing him back, pushing into him. "I'm sorry, okay? That was a shitty joke. I'll come. Of course I'll come."

He relaxed. "You will?"

"Yeah," I said, gripping his arm, feeling high. "I'll be there."

36.

I got there at five past six and rang the bell. I wore a dress—my *only* dress—pale blue, sheer, and sleeveless. Over that I wore a slim cardigan and my parka.

"Hey, you." Fred. He had on a holey sweater vest and his favorite cords.

"You look nice," I said, undoing my coat and dropping it onto the upholstered chair in the foyer.

"You too—your dress." He touched my upper arm gently. "You want anything?" He looked uneasy—glassy-eyed and drunk, maybe. "Adina hasn't started cooking yet."

"I'm fine," I said, following Fred past the den into the kitchen. Adina sat on a high chair at the end of the island drinking wine from a tumbler.

"You're sure? You want wine? We can open another bottle."

"Let's," said Adina, downing the last of it while pulling a

second off the rack on the hutch. "You look like you could use a drink, Katonah."

I shut my eyes for a sec, steeling myself—and when I reopened them, Fred was passing me a glass.

"Thanks." I took a sip.

"Hey, D."

"Mm?" Her hair was tangled and her sleepy eyes, muddied with kohl.

"What happened to your Peruvian feast?"

"I'm not cooking," she said. I wondered if she'd smeared her makeup on purpose. "Your girlfriend's all dressed up—don't disappoint, she looks hungry."

"I'm fine," I whispered.

"It's okay," Fred said, hurrying to the pantry, pulling out pasta, jarred sauce, and pots. "I'll cook, no biggie."

"I don't need to eat anything," I said, sounding shrill. My hands trembled. "I just—" I wanted it over with. I wanted to say my piece before dinner and drinks dulled my nerve. "Are we gonna talk about what happened or not?"

She looked up. "Why, what happened? Did you two do it, finally?"

"Adina."

"What? What's the big deal? You guys are big prudes. You probably fuck with your eyes closed."

"Adina!" shrieked Fred.

"What? What're you looking at?" She was talking to

me, not him. "God, I'm so sick of your flat little face."

My eyes flooded. My cheeks felt on fire. I turned away, walked to the living room, sat down on the couch, and cried. I missed Evie. Why was I here?

"Hey." This came moments later. "Hey, look at me," Fred said. A hand touched my head. I looked up. Both of them hovered above.

"I'm sorry," said Adina. Her expression was blank but she sounded remorseful.

"What else?" nudged Fred.

"I didn't mean what I said about your face."

I wiped my wet nose with the back of my wrist.

"And what else?" continued Fred. "What about the rumor? The kiss?"

She looked at him. "That wasn't me."

"You're lying."

"I'm not," she said. "I told one person we kissed." Her eyes shot back to me. "The story got twisted."

She's lying. She never stops. "Adina," I said.

"Don't say my name that way."

"What way?"

"Like you hate me. Like I'm your enemy. I'm not."

"Adina," I said again. "*We* didn't kiss. You, like, attacked me."

"Fine, whatever, *I* kissed *you*. It was nice, right? You liked it?"

I searched Fred's face. Was she crazy?

She smiled at me. "Wait here, okay? I'll go get the open bottle and some snacks."

She wandered away, back toward the kitchen. Fred sat down next to me. "You're weirded out."

"She's *out* of her fucking mind."

"She's not, she's just—her perspective is skewed." Would it *never* end? Would he *ever* quit defending her?

"She's a fucking anorexic. Maybe if she ate something every once in a while, she'd stay sane."

"She's not—she eats. She's picky."

He couldn't possibly be *that* naive. "Are you blind?"

Fred recoiled. "*No*, I'm not blind."

"And her drinking—"

"We *all* drink."

"Not like that, we don't." Silence. Death stares. "I think I should go."

Fred recanted. "No, no, Alex, don't. Please." He took my hand. "You're right, okay? You're right, I just—we all have to get along."

"Why? Why do we all have to get along?"

"Because. She's my sister. Stay, please?" His hand was hot. "Just drink something and stay? I'll make us dinner. I can cook, I swear it." His lashes fluttered. "Come on, you wore your dress."

I had, but why? Tonight had been a waste of good clothes.

"Please," Fred pleaded. *"Please."* He kissed me. His lips tasted like ChapStick and tobacco.

"Okay," I said, relenting.

"Yeah? Is that a yes?"

I nodded.

"Good." He bit his thumbnail. "You won't be sorry, I swear it."

We'd finished one bottle and started another. My second, Adina's third. She was piss drunk, hanging upside down off the side of the sofa, laughing and braiding a long lock of hair.

"You guys look really great this way. All flipped around." She righted herself. "Anyone want a peanut?" She thrust a plastic bag with five unshelled nuts in my face.

Fred took the bag.

I wasn't sure why I'd stayed. Drunk Adina was only a fraction more pleasant than sober Adina. "I have candy in my car," I offered. "I should get it." We still hadn't eaten. I stood, feeling woozy.

"No thanks," she said. Then: "Let's play a game."

"I'll be back in two secs—"

"No, now." She pulled me down by my dress hem. Fred winced. "Sit." She pushed on her teeth with two fingers. "Truth or dare."

"Adina." Fred.

"What?" And then, to me: "Truth or dare, Katonah?"

"I don't—I don't know. I don't really care."

"Sure you do. You care about everything. Pick one."

"I— Truth."

"Alex, you don't have to—"

"Shut up," she snapped at Fred. "Truth, great, I love it." Then, sounding upbeat and impish: "Tell me about your secret relationship with my brother."

"There's no secret relationship."

"You've been together, I know you have." She stuck her chin out.

"We haven't."

"Come on, tell me what it's like, with Fred."

Instant nausea. I looked at Fred, who wasn't moving. "Please stop," he said softly.

"Stop what?"

"Interrogating her. She's telling the truth, we haven't done anything."

"You're lying to me," she insisted, suddenly seeming so pissed. "I don't ever lie to you. I don't keep things from you."

"Once, okay? We kissed once."

She paused to chew a hangnail. "Like how?"

He looked up. "Like, how people kiss, Adina. Like a kiss, I dunno."

"Like a peck?"

"I don't know."

"Show me."

I froze, my eyes darting between twins. "No," I blurted, getting up on my knees.

"I was talking to him, freak, not you."

I winced as if I'd been hit. Fred kept his head down as Adina drunkenly inched her way closer. "Show me," she repeated.

"No."

"Show me." She hovered nearby, taunting him.

"Adina." He straightened up, swinging his hand, intending to push her away.

"Come on, show me," she said, catching his wrist. "I want to see."

"Let go."

"No."

"Come on, quit it—let *go*."

She kissed him. Like a girl might kiss a boy. One forceful, angry, little kiss. It lasted seconds but I swear, seemed like forever—me, frozen in disbelief and Fred, swatting and squirming like a caged cat.

"We're even," she said to me when it was through. Both watched me, looking startled. Their mouths matched—both splotchy and red.

"Fuck." After a quiet moment or two, came the squall. "What the *fuck* was that? What's *wrong* with you?" Fred stood quickly, tripping in place.

I watched Adina. I felt dreamy. Disbelieving. She seemed so frail now, hunched over, drunk. Banana circled her, meowing madly, pawing at her knees.

Fred to me: "Are you coming?"

I got up.

37.

We sat in the dark by the river, away from the Bishop house.

"You okay?"

Stupidly cold but, "Yeah."

"You want to go back to the car?"

I mimed *no*, then wrapped my arms around my waist, bending forward. Fred threw a pebble into the water. It skipped twice, then sank. "We used to come here a lot as kids. She loved this place."

I picked a rock off the ground and rolled it between two fingers. What had changed? How had a kid who loved rivers and Audubon walks turned into such a malevolent freak?

"What're you thinking?" Fred asked.

Why did I want to be a part of this? Something so insular and weird? "What do you think I'm thinking?"

He touched my hands, then the ends of my hair. I flashed

on Audrey, two towns over, in field hockey goggles and cleats. "Your girlfriend. She moved."

"Her dad changed jobs."

"Are you lying?"

He looked hurt. I leaned over and scooped up a handful dirt.

"What's that for?"

"This?" I held up my hand, inspecting it. The mud felt nice—heavy, cool. I squeezed it through my fingers and shook my hand clean. "Have you been with lots of other people?"

"Other people?"

"Like, other girls. Not Audrey. I know about Audrey." I straightened up. "Adina says you've been with lots of other girls. That you're a cheater. Is that true?"

"Like, that I've slept with other girls?"

"Yeah."

"That I cheated on Audrey?"

"Mmhmm."

"Adina said that?"

I nodded.

"No, that's not true." I believed him. He looked so hopeless.

"Come home with me?" I wanted that feeling back. The one from Grams's porch. "Please?"

"Yeah, of course I'll come."

I grabbed Fred's hand.

* * *

We didn't do anything. We just lay there, side by side, fully dressed, not sleeping. Fred stroked my hair and I rubbed his feet with my feet. We talked about dumb stuff, crap we hated and shitty books and stuff, and then around two, Adina texted: *Where are you?* She texted twice, then called. Fred sat up. He watched his phone flash.

"Don't answer it. Please," I pleaded. I wouldn't let her wreck this. "Not now, okay? Everything's so nice right now."

He smiled at me. He dropped his phone to the floor and curled an arm around my shoulders and chest. He'd chosen me. For once, it was me and not her. I backed into him, feeling like I'd won some shiny prize. "Thanks," I murmured, and Fred yanked the blankets tight, overhead. We stayed that way, under the covers, until it got hot and too hard to breathe. Later, when it was nearly light, Fred told me he'd had sex only once, with Audrey Glick. And that afterward she refused to touch him, and eventually they just stopped talking.

"I've never had sex with anyone," I said.

"That's okay." He drew circles on my shoulder with his pinky nail.

Six-fifty-four a.m., Fred's cell again.

I leaned over the edge of the bed, sweeping the floor for his phone. *Jesus, Adina, get a boyfriend who's not your brother.* I checked the ID screen. "Oh. Hey." I shook Fred. "Your dad."

Fred sat up, groggy. He took the phone. "Hello?" His cheeks changed shades. Pink to white.

"Something wrong?"

He waved me away. "Okay," he said, folding his phone shut. Then, to me: "She crashed Dad's car."

"What?"

"They found an empty fifth of vodka on the floor of his Mercedes."

"When?"

"I dunno."

"Well, where is she?"

"St. Mary's."

"Is she okay?"

His face was blank. "I dunno."

My heart went nuts—racing, skipping beats. "What do you mean, *you don't know*? He must have said something."

"They had to pump her stomach."

"Is she conscious?"

He looked confused. He opened his mouth but no sound came out. Then: "I don't know."

"He didn't say?"

"I don't know." I could hear him breathing. He pushed me sideways and stood up.

"I'm coming with you."

"No, you have to stay."

"Why?"

"Just—*stay*, please?" He rubbed one eye. "I'll call, okay?" He grabbed his keys off my nightstand.

"Wait."

"What?"

"I'm sorry," I said.

"For what?" He seemed legitimately perplexed. "I'll call you," he said again. Then he walked out the door.

38.

"Babe, eat something." Mom and I sat on the porch, wrapped in blankets. A dish of dry toast lay in my lap.

"I don't want it."

"You have to eat." This from a woman who hadn't eaten a solid meal in more than three months. "Come on, two bites; you'll feel better."

I picked the dish up and placed it on the ground next to my cold tea. I eyed my phone. I'd tried Fred twenty times in the last hour. It was quarter to eleven. I was ready to implode.

"Babe."

"What?"

"I can drive you to St. Mary's."

"He doesn't want me there. He asked me to stay away."

"Okay." Mom's eyes widened. "You're sure he meant it?"

"Yeah. *Yes.*" I rubbed my face and last night's makeup rubbed off on my hand.

"You sure you don't want a bath? If he calls, I'll come get you."

"I'm fine," I said, only I wasn't. "Let's not talk, okay?" I was terrified and could not stop picturing Adina slumped over the steering wheel with her head bashed in.

My cell rang.

"Oh, shit!" I screamed. *"Shit."* I fumbled nervously for my phone. This was it—Adina was dead, or brain-dead, or comatose, I knew it. Fred would be devastated. He'd blame me. I'd destroyed his life, after all.

"Hello?" I was panting. I sounded completely deranged.

"She's okay."

"Oh God."

"Alex?"

"Yeah, I'm here, I'm just—" I laughed. My body loosened. "Really relieved."

"Her head's pretty bad. She whacked it on the driver's side window and her chest is bruised from the air bag."

"But she's fine?"

"I mean, yeah, she's alive." He sounded distant and weird. "She, like, poisoned herself then drove into a tree."

I looked at my mother, who was watching me with a hand to her heart.

"Is she awake?"

"Yeah."

"Can she go home?"

"They're keeping her overnight. They want to do a psych eval."

"Why?"

"Why?" he repeated.

Stupid, stupid, stupid, Alex. "Sorry. You need anything?"

"I'm okay. I'm gonna go home now and shower."

"Call me later?" No response. I heard clanking in the background. Metal on metal, maybe? And a man's voice. Deep, and sad sounding. "Or I could call you?"

"Alex, my dad's here."

"No, of course."

"I'll call later."

"Yeah, but—tell Adina I'm glad she's okay?"

Click.

39.

Friday. A creepy hush followed me from class to class. Everyone silent and staring. I'd heard two conflicting rumors: Adina had swallowed a bottle of pills, some liquor, and crashed her Dad's car on purpose. *Botched suicide attempt by freak anorexic.* The second story was softer*: It was accidental, she's so small—too much booze, poor little girl.* I hadn't even considered the worst, but Charlotte insisted: "She's so goddamn skinny—what's the difference? Starve yourself or drink a shit-ton and drive into a tree? I mean, really. And you know about their mom, don't you?"

Forth block. We were outside, on the lawn. Charlotte had a free period. I was skipping phys ed.

"She's dead, I know."

"No, you know how she died, right?"

I shrugged.

"Car wreck."

"So?"

"So? Seriously, who drives into a tree?"

"She was drunk."

"That girl is bat-shit crazy." She mashed her lips together. "Admit it."

"Admit *what*?" I was picking apart a blade of new grass.

"That maybe she drove into that tree on purpose." She pulled a pack of Tic Tacs from her jeans pocket. "Want one?"

"No."

"I don't understand why you're so nice to her." She shook out a handful of orange candy. "She's not very nice to you."

"Who says?"

"Alex."

I wasn't sure why I felt the need to defend and protect. Charlotte was right—Adina was awful. Still: "If it's true, if she did do what she did on purpose . . . I dunno." I rubbed one eye. "That's just sad, don't you think? That makes me really, really sad."

Charlotte swallowed. "Well now I feel bad."

"Yeah?"

"I really do."

I smiled. I felt my first ever genuine swell of warmth toward her.

"What?" she asked. "What's with the look?"

"You have a heart after all. Who knew?"

She chucked a Tic Tac at my face. "Shut up," she said. "I keep it hidden."

40.

"We broke up." Evie in the rain. "He broke up with me." Her sopping sweatshirt hung off one shoulder. "Al!" she cried, her words punctuated by spastic gulps of air.

"Jesus, Evie." Her wailing gutted me. "I'm so sorry," I said, pulling her inside.

"He—he said—he said he wasn't sure he loved me."

"Oh, Eves." I blotted her down with two damp dish towels. "You look like you've been swimming,"

Footsteps, then Mom, arms open.

"I'm soaked."

"Don't care."

They embraced. I dropped the towels in the sink and grabbed the kettle off the stove. "You want anything?"

Evie smiled and pulled away from my mother. "Tea, yeah." She yanked her sweatshirt overhead, then stood shivering, half-naked, in her black cotton bra. "Can I borrow something?"

I filled the kettle, switched on the gas, and grabbed Evie's shirt. "We'll stick this in the dryer—but, here." I grabbed a clean tee off the laundry pile. "Have this."

"I feel like I'm dying," she said.

"I know, babe." Mom slipped my shirt over Evie's wet head. "It's terrible, right? That feeling?"

Evie nodded.

"You'll be fine, though. You'll forget how this feels, I promise." Mom's eyes went wet.

"I won't."

"You will," she insisted, running a towel through Evie's thick, matted bob. "You'll love again," she said, planting a kiss on Evie's round, ruddy cheek. "I guarantee it."

We lay on the floor in my room.

"I hate this thing," Evie said, still crying, clutching my afghan. "It's itchy."

"So don't touch it."

"Don't be mean."

"I'm not," I said, rolling toward her. "I'm not being mean." But maybe I was. A piece of me felt glad Ben was gone. Evie was mine again. "I'm sorry."

"I just don't get it. He didn't even seem upset. 'I'm not sure I love you.' How can that be true?"

I had no clue. How was it possible to love someone who didn't love you back? *I should ask Dad,* I thought. *Or Fred.* "Did you tell Judith?"

"No."

"She doesn't know you're here?"

"Uh-uh."

I grabbed the phone off my nightstand.

"What are you doing?"

"I'm calling your mom."

"No."

"She needs to know you're here, Eves. Once she realizes you're gone, she'll freak." I dialed.

"Stop." She dove for the phone. "Gimme," she said, taking hold. "I'll talk." And, after a bit, to Judith: "It's me." Heavy sigh. "I'm in Meadow Marsh with Alex and Liz. I'm sleeping here, okay?" She took another deep, broken breath. "I'll go. I swear I'll go. I'll leave here at six and be back before homeroom." A beat. "Well, what do you expect me to do, drive back now in the rain?" Another pause. "Okay. Okay, okay. Me too." She flipped my phone shut. "Alex."

"What."

"I'm sad."

"I know," I said. "Come'ere."

She flung herself forward, folding up in my arms.

41.

"So, I'm thinking."

"About what?"

We were on the porch, Mom and me, eating M&M's and drinking root beer from glass bottles. Mom had her heels kicked up on Grams's old wicker patio table. I clutched my cell. Fred hadn't called since the morning of the accident. One week. I'd been relentlessly nauseated.

"About selling the house."

I sat up. "Seriously?"

"Yeah. It's not really ours, you know?"

"Right, but"—I ate an M&M—"we sell the house and go where?"

Somewhere that's ours." When Grams died Mom hadn't wanted to weed through Grams's things, let alone find a buyer.

"Around here?"

"Yeah. We stay close to Dad. You finish out this year and next. We put the place up for sale and start looking for someplace new. Fresh start." She pushed some hair behind one ear. "Someplace that feels like *us*."

I thought about it. Brand-new life with Mom. What would that even look like? Sunny kitchen? Sobriety? Waffle Sundays? "What about Grams's stuff?"

"We keep what we want. But the rest—" She looked back at the house. "I dunno. Sell it?"

I took a long swig of soda and looked at our lawn. Brown and sparse with a few bits of new, green growth. "Apartment or house?"

"House."

"Rental or what, we buy something new?"

"We rent, I think. For now."

I stood up and put one foot flat against the porch railing. "Do I get to help decorate?"

"Absolutely."

I smiled. "Well okay, then."

"Okay?"

"Yeah. Why not."

Mom grinned. We clanked bottles. "Cheers," she said.

"L'chaim."

"How are you?"

"Skinny." Eves sounded far away. "Eating is impossible.

Anything but crackers and apples makes me ralph."

"Sorry," I said, switching ears, swinging my feet over the gearshift and into the passenger-side seat. I was parked outside school. Three p.m. Another day, no Fred.

"It's fine. Heartbreak diet. My boobs will just continue to wither. Eventually they'll look like yours."

I tried to laugh but no sound came out.

"Hello? Al? You there? I was kidding."

"No, I know."

"You okay?"

I put two fingers to my lips and inhaled. Fake dragging off my fake cigarette. "Did I tell you that Adina Bishop got into a car accident?"

"What? When?"

"Two weeks ago."

"*Shit*, Al. Is she okay?"

"Yeah, she's okay." I told her about the vodka and the tree and the stitches. "I haven't seen Fred since."

"Why not?"

"Don't know."

"Did something happen?

Yep: Adina kissed me, I kissed Fred, Adina kissed Fred, then she drove into a tree. "I—not really."

"You're sure?"

"Yeah." Saying it all out loud, reliving the saga, seemed exhausting. I wasn't even sure why I'd brought it up.

"And why would you wait two weeks to tell me Adina Bishop nearly killed herself?"

I stiffened. "Killed herself? No—"

"I meant—you know what I meant. What's wrong with you? You sound miserable."

"I'm okay," I said, forcing a smile, hoping my voice sounded bright. "I didn't tell you because, well, there wasn't really much to tell."

"I don't believe you," she said.

"Yeah, I know you don't." I fiddled with the knob on my stereo.

"You into this?" Mom held up two plates from a checkered cream and black dish set.

"No, I like the floral."

"Which ones?"

"The plates with the pink tulips? And there's a creamer and teapot that goes with."

"Okay, I'm selling these, then." Mom set the stack of checkered china on the dining room hutch. I went back to weeding through cookbooks and novels, encyclopedias and biographies. "Can I keep this stuff?"

Mom looked up. "What stuff?"

"Her books."

"Which ones?"

"All of them."

She let out a sigh. "Al, please, find something to get rid of. Books are heavy and hard to move. . . ." She went back to her dishware. I surveyed the house—tall piles of kitchen crap, wall art, electrical gadgets, faux jewels, lamps, tagged furniture. Grams had been gone three years, but this was the first time I really felt sad. All she'd ever owned, for sale. Years of accumulated *stuff*—some of it meaningful, some of it useless—would now mean something new to someone else.

The screen door rattled, then squeaked. "Hello?" A boy's voice. "Katonah?" *Fred.*

"We're back here!" I shouted, instantly breaking a sweat.

"Who's that?" Mom whispered.

Fred. Fred in the dining room, dressed in brown.

"Hi."

"Hello."

My fingertips tingled.

"Mommy, Fred. Fred, my mother." I gestured back and forth between them both. Mom took off her glasses, stood, and shook Fred's hand. "Liz."

"Finally." Then: "Wow, the place is—"

"A mess, we know. Estate sale this weekend. And the move—did Alex tell you?"

He looked at me. "You're leaving?"

"No. I mean, yeah, we're selling Grams's, but we're staying. In Meadow Marsh."

He exhaled.

Mom: "Okay, more boxes. And tape." She slid between two stacks of plates and grabbed her keys off the table.

"You're going?" I asked.

"I'll be back in an hour with packing supplies." She smiled. "Take a break, okay? Get your friend some tea." She patted my head on her way to the door.

I looked at Fred. "You want tea?"

The screen door slammed. "Um." We were alone.

"We have green, Oolong, white . . ."

"I'm okay."

I glanced toward the pantry. "Snack?"

"No thanks." He shoved his hands into his pockets.

"You can sit," I said, a knot in my gut the size of a grapefruit.

He sat on the arm of the sofa. I stayed standing, my shoulders and head against the wall. "How's Adina?"

His head shot up. "She's okay. She's home."

"Are you guys coming back to school?"

"I am. Tomorrow." His glanced sideways. "D's taking some time off."

"What for?"

"She's . . . weighing her options."

"Oh, uh-huh."

He picked my old rag doll up off the floor.

"That's Dolly," I said.

"What's she doing down here?"

"She—" I grabbed her back, blushing. "She got lost."

Then: "You didn't return any of my calls." The second I said it, I regretted it.

Fred looked like he might stand, but instead, stayed put. "Any, like, house leads?"

Ignore me, sure. "There's a place off Chester Hill that Mom likes. It's small, but the attic's been refurbished. I could sleep there."

"In the attic?"

"Yeah."

Fred got up. He walked forward. I pushed my heel against the power socket. "Sorry," I said. My voice broke.

"What for?"

I looked down at my hands, which were shaking. "I feel really guilty about what happened with Adina."

"*You* feel guilty?"

"You know what people are saying?"

"Alex."

"No, have you heard?"

He took my hands.

"That she did it on purpose."

"Alex."

"What? Are you hearing me?"

"Yeah, I hear you. Sorry I didn't call."

I squeezed his fingers hard. "What's wrong with you? Why won't you talk to me?"

"About? Why, what do you want to know?"

"How'd your mom die?"

Without missing a beat: "Car accident."

"Well, what about Adina?" I shifted back and forth. "Did she do what she did—did she do it on purpose?"

He shrugged. "I don't know."

My vison blurred.

"Hey." He crouched down, so our faces were level. "Why the tears?"

"That's—that's so fucked up." I was huffing. "Why would she do that? Because I'm like, *taking* you? Because I like, *stole* you from her?"

"Hey." He grabbed my head, pulling me close. "Stop it. Stop crying. This has nothing to do with you."

I pulled back so I could look at him. "Nothing?"

"Adina has her own shit going on." His brow furrowed. "This isn't about you. *Or* me. Besides, she doesn't want to die. She wants attention."

"Really?"

"Yeah. Really."

I wiped my nose and my cheeks. "Sorry."

"Again?" He smiled. "What now?"

"I made it about *me*."

"Alex, come on, stop." He leaned forward just an inch. Our noses grazed. "I know what I'm doing," he said, quietly. He kissed my neck. Then right behind my ear. Then the corners of my mouth and lastly, my lips. I didn't move or kiss back. I stayed very still, letting him touch my hands, my hips, the sides of my face.

"You're sure about this?" I whispered into him.

"Yeah," he said, pulling back a bit. "I am."

42.

Day trip to Dad's. I didn't call ahead or ask if I was welcome—I just went.

"I'm gonna pack up some stuff, okay?"

Caroline and I stood face-to-face in the den downstairs. She lifted a tissue to her nose and blew. "That's fine."

"Where's my dad?"

"Hardware store."

"Are you sick?"

She shrugged, wiping her nose. "Allergies. Or, I dunno, a cold, maybe? I'm fine." She looked messy and vulnerable. I felt a flicker of sympathy.

"When Dad gets back, tell him I'm upstairs, packing?"

Chicken was at my heels, licking and nipping and softly panting.

"Sure," Caroline said. Then: "Alex, hey."

I stopped.

"You need anything?"

"Like what?"

"I don't know. Water? Food?"

I continued up the steps. "I've lived here sixteen years," I said. "I think I can handle my own drinks and snacks."

I didn't pack everything. Just the crap I couldn't live without: photo albums, a clear plastic bin stuffed with summer clothes, my favorite floral lamp with the hand-painted shade, a big barrel curling iron, a framed shot of Chicken at the beach playing ball, my dad's old bathrobe.

"Hi, kid."

"Oh." Dad. I was mid-pack, clutching his bathrobe.

"That mine?"

"Not anymore," I said, shoving it deep into my duffel.

He smiled. "Need any help?"

"I'm pretty much done." I picked up the last of it. A stack of summer tees. Plastic bin overflow.

"We didn't ski this year."

"Nope."

I yanked on the bag zipper.

"Alex."

"What?"

"Come'ere, please?"

"Why?" I wasn't going to hug him, like him, kiss him, forgive him.

"Just come here. This'll take two secs."

I stood, wobbling forward. "Okay," I said, facing him. "What?"

He wound his arms around my shoulders. "Love you," he said, squeezing tight.

Fuck, fuck, fuck it. With zero fanfare, after four months, I surrendered. "Me too."

Forty minutes later I stood on the smooth cement driveway, loading my trunk.

Chicken nudged my kneecaps. "Sweet girl," I cooed. She jumped up, patting my shoulders with her fat, fuzzy paws. "You gonna miss me?"

She whined. Licked my cheek. Nuzzled my ear. I laughed.

"You going?"

It was Caroline. Wiping her hands on a dish towel and walking forward.

"Yeah." I stood up.

She nodded and pressed her lips together. "Well, it was good seeing you. Even briefly."

"Thanks."

"Next weekend?"

I shook my head. "Next weekend with Mom." I waved, then gave Chicken one last pat. I reached for my door.

"Hey, Alex."

"Hmm?"

We stood a foot apart. "I just—I want to say something to you."

I waited.

"I know how you feel about me," she said, licking her lips and glancing right. "I can only imagine what you must think of my relationship with your father."

I try not to think about your relationship with my father.

"I just—please understand, I don't like hurting you, *or* your mother. . . . But I love your dad. And I'm sorry. About the mess, you know?"

The mess. The mess, yes, I *did* know. I felt a quick, unexpected flash of compassion, then, as quickly as it came, it went. "Okay," I said, making a face. "Is that all?" I readjusted my bag.

"Yeah, that's it," she said. She lifted a hand, shielding her eyes from the sun. "See you soon?"

I slid behind the wheel, shut my car door, and rolled down the window. "Yeah," I said. It was nice out. Breezy sixties. Bright. "See you soon," I said, starting the car.

43.

It looked different now, their house. Less stately, more broken-down and sad. I followed the path leading up to the front door and pushed the bell.

"Oh. Hi."

I had a date. I was on the dot. "Adina." She looked small and pale. Limp hair, no makeup. Young and meek in her yellow cotton robe. "How are you?"

"Fine." Her voice broke but her face didn't move.

"How's your head?" She had a stylish line of stitches sewn into her hairline.

"It's nothing."

"It looks painful."

"It's fine," she said. She screamed for her brother.

"Coming!" Fred's voice sounded small and far away. Adina and I watched each other for several seconds, waiting. I wasn't sure what to say: *I hate you, I'm sorry, I hate you, I'm sorry*? I felt mixed up and mad and a tad regretful. Adina, though, was still Adina.

"When are you coming back to school?"

"Not sure." Her lip twitched.

"Hi." Fred strode forward looking shiny and clean. He passed Adina, then lunged for me, pulling me into a snug embrace.

"Hi," I whispered.

"Big night out?" she asked.

Fred grabbed his keys off the armoire and glanced backward, only briefly. "Big night out, yeah." He rested a hand on my back, sending a victorious blast up my spine. "Don't wait up," Fred said easily, ushering me quickly out the door.

44.

May.

Evie and I were in my new room, tacking paint swatches to the moldings and walls.

"He's skinny."

Mom and I had settled on the house with the refurbished attic. 633 Memory Lane. Small. White colonial. Right off Chester Hill.

"What's wrong with skinny?" I held a violet swatch up to my eyelet bedspread.

"Did I *say* skinny was bad?" Evie's new guy, of course. There was *always* a new guy. "*You're* skinny."

I wasn't. "I'm not." I'd been eating like mad for a month. Ever since Adina's breakdown I'd sworn off starvation. Since, clearly, hunger = psychosis.

"How's about this one?" She waved her finger at a swatch

constellation. "The yellow. Hand it to me. What's the color code?"

I peeled the swatch off the wall. "Five four two zero zero. What is it with you and yellow?"

"Hmm?"

Evie's room was a pale butter. "Your walls, *my* walls . . ."

She finished scribbling down the numbers and looked up. "It's superior. Very calming." She gestured to the window molding. "Cream, right? Numbers please?"

"Six eleven three zero eight." I squeezed between my mattress and Grams's boxed book collection and collapsed on the wood floor next to Evie. "It'll be nice, right?"

"Better than nice." She shouldered me. "You'll need curtains."

"Mom's making some with Grams's old lace."

Evie gazed past me to my wide, wicker headboard. "What're we doing after this?"

I heard birds and Weedwackers and cars on roads. "Diner dinner."

"Gross."

I looked left. At a tall stack of blue swatches, beckoning. "Hey, Eves?"

"Hey what?"

I smiled. I watched my clean, blank white wall. Wondered about this one little circular crack in the upper left-hand corner near my ceiling—how it got there, and what it would look like once it'd been patched with a little plaster and painted a pretty, brand-new periwinkle blue.

Acknowledgments

Anica Rissi, thank you. You are a fantastic editor and a stellar human being.

Jen Rofé, you're top-notch.

Fine people at Simon Pulse, I appreciate, *endlessly*, all you do.

Adeline, Alisa, Milly, Amanda, Margaret, Justine, Jade, Anna, Jordan, Jenna: You talk me off writerly cliffs.

2k9-ers, without you this past year would've been one long freak-out. Thanks for holding my hand in the dark.

Friends, fam: I'm the luckiest. Much gratitude for the unrelenting support and encouragement.

FROM

Nothing Like You

BY LAUREN STRASNICK

We were parked at Point Dume, Paul and I, the two of us tangled together, half dressed, half not. Paul's car smelled like sea air and stale smoke, and from his rearview hung a yellow and pink plastic lanyard that swayed with the breeze drifting in through the open car window. I hung on to Paul, thinking, *I like your face, I love your hands, let's do this, let's do this, let's do this*, one arm locked around the back of his head, the other wedged between two scratched-up leather seat cushions, bracing myself against the pain while wondering, idly, if this feels any different when you love the person or when you do it lying down on a bed.

This was the same beach where I'd spent millions of mornings with my mother, wading around at low tide searching for sea anemone and orange and purple starfish. It had cliffs and crashing waves and seemed like the appropriate place to do something utterly unoriginal, like lose my virginity in the backseat of some guy's dinged-up, bright red BMW.

I didn't really know Paul but that didn't really matter. There we were, making sappy, sandy memories on the Malibu Shore, fifteen miles from home. It was nine p.m. on a school night. I needed to be back by ten.

"That was nice," he said, dragging a hand down the back of my head through my hair.

"Mm," I nodded, not really sure what to say back. I hadn't realized the moment was over, but there it was—our unceremonious end. "It's getting late, right?" I dragged my jeans over my lap. "Maybe you should take me home?"

"Yeah, absolutely," Paul shimmied backward, buttoning his pants. "I'll get you home." He wrinkled his nose, smiled, then swung his legs over the armrest and into the driver's side seat.

"Thanks," I said, trying my best to seem casual and upbeat, hiking my underwear and jeans back on, then creeping forward so we were seated side by side.

"You ready?" he asked, pinching an unlit cigarette between his bottom and top teeth.

"Sure thing." I buckled my seat belt and watched Paul run the head of a Zippo against the side seam on his pants, igniting a tiny flame. I turned my head toward the window and pressed my nose against the glass. There, in the not-so-far-off distance, an orange glow lit the sky, gleaming bright. *Brushfire.*

"Remind me, again?" He jangled his car keys.

"Hillside. Off Topanga Canyon."

"Right, sorry." He lit his cigarette and turned the ignition. "I'm shit with directions."

Chapter 2

Topanga was burning.

Helicopters swarmed overhead dumping water and red glop all over fiery shrubs and mulch. The air tasted sour and chalky and my eyes and throat burned from the blaze. Flaming hills, thick smoke—this used to seriously freak me out. Now, though, I sort of liked it. My whole town tinted orange and smelling like barbecue and burnt pine needles.

I was standing in my driveway, Harry's leash wrapped twice around my wrist. We watched the smoke rise and billow behind my house and I thought: *This is what nuclear war must look like. Mushroom clouds and raining ash*. I bent down, kissed Harry's dry nose, and scratched hard behind his ears. "One quick walk," I said. "Just down the hill and back."

He barked.

We sped through the canyon. Past tree swings and chopped wood and old RVs parked on lawns. Past the plank bridge that crosses the dried-out ravine, the Topanga Christian Fellowship with its peeling blue and white sign, the Christian Science Church, the Topanga Equestrian Center with the horses on the hill and the fancy veggie restaurant down below in their shadow. That day, the horses were indoors, shielded from the muddy, smoky air. Harry and I U-turned at the little hippie gift shop attached to the fancy veggie restaurant, and started back up the hill to my house.

Barely anyone was out on the road. It was dusky out, almost dark, so we ran the rest of the way home. I let Harry off his leash once we'd reached my driveway, then followed him around back to The Shack.

"Knock, knock," I said, rattling the flimsy tin door and pushing my way in. Nils was lying on his side reading an old issue of *National Geographic*. I kicked off my sneakers and dropped Harry's leash on the ground, flinging myself down next to Nils and onto the open futon.

"Anything good?" I asked, grabbing the magazine from between his fingertips.

"Fruit bats," he said, grabbing it back.

I shivered and rolled sideways, butting my head against his back.

"You cold?" he asked.

"No," I said. "Just a chill . . ."

He rolled over and looked at me. My eyes settled on his nose: long and straight and reassuring. "You freaked about the fire?" he asked.

I shrugged.

"They've got it all pretty much contained, you know. 'Least last time I checked."

I grabbed a pillow off the floor and used it to prop up my head. Harry was sniffing around at my toes, licking and nibbling at my pinkie nail. I laughed.

"What?" said Nils. "What's so funny?"

"Just Harry." I shook my head.

"No, come on, what?"

I grabbed his magazine back. "Fruit bats," I squealed, holding open the page with the fuzzy flying rodents. "I want one, okay? This year, for my birthday."

"Sure thing, princess." He moved closer to me, curling his legs to his chest. "Anything you say."

Nils is my oldest friend. My next-door neighbor. This shack has been ours since we were ten. It was my dad's toolshed for about forty-five minutes—before Nils and I met, and took over. The Shack is its new name, given a ways back on my sixteenth birthday. Years ten through fifteen, we called it Clubhouse. Nils thought The Shack sounded much more grown up. I agree. The Shack has edge.

"Have you done all your reading for Kiminski's quiz tomorrow?"

"No" I said, flipping the page.

"Where were you last night, anyway? I came by but Jeff said you were out."

Jeff is my dad, FYI. "I just went down to the beach for a bit."

"Alone?" Nils asked.

"Yeah, alone," I lied, dropping Nils's magazine and flipping onto my side.

Nils didn't need to know about Paul Bennett or any other boy in my life. Nils had, at that point, roughly five new girlfriends each week. I'd stopped asking questions.

"Hols, should we study?"

"Put on Jethro Tull for two secs. We can study in a bit." The weeks prior to this Nils and I had spent sorting through my mother's entire music collection, organizing all her old records, tapes, and CDs into categories on a shelf Jeff had built for The Shack.

"This song sucks," shouted Nils over the first few bars of "Aqualung." I raised one hand high in the air, rocking along while scanning her collection for other tapes we might like.

"Hols?"

"Yeah?"

"Your mom had shit taste in music."

I squinted. "You *so* know you love it. Admit it. You *love* Jethro Tull."

"I do. I love Jethro Tull." He was looking at me. His eyes looked kind of misty. *Don't say it, Nils, please don't say it.* "I miss your mom." He said it.

I sat up. "Buck up, little boy. She's watching us from a happy little cloud in the sky, okay?"

He tugged at my hair. "How come you never get sad, Holly? I think it's weird you don't ever get sad."

"I *do* get sad." I stood, dusting some dirt off my butt. "Just because you don't see it doesn't mean it isn't there."

Chapter 3

School.

7:44 a.m. and I was rushing down the hall toward World History with my coffee sloshing everywhere and one lock of sopping wet hair whipping me in the face. I got one "Hey," and two or three half-smiles from passersby right before sliding into my seat just as the bell went *ding ding ding.*

Ms. Stein was set to go with her number two pencil, counting heads, ". . . sixteen, seventeen . . . who's missing? Saskia? You here? Has anyone seen Saskia?" As if on cue, Saskia Van Wyck came racing through the door, *clickity-clack* in her shiny black flats, plopping down in the empty seat to my left. "I'm here, sorry! I'm right here," she said, dragging the back of her hand dramatically across her brow. *Adorable.* I slurped my coffee.

“Take out your books, people. Let’s read until eight fifteen, then we’ll discuss chapters nine and ten. ’Kay?”

I pulled my book from my bag and glanced to my left.

Saskia Van Wyck. Paul Bennett’s girlfriend-slash-ex-girlfriend. I barely knew her. I only knew that she was skinny, pretty, marginally popular, and lived in this old adobe house just off the PCH, wedged right in between my favorite Del Taco and the old crappy gas station on Valley View Drive. I’d been there once, in sixth grade, for a birthday party, where no more than four kids showed up, but I remembered things: her turquoise blue bedroom walls. An avocado tree. A naked Barbie and a stuffed brown bear she kept hidden under her twin wrought-iron bed.

Saskia leaned toward me. “Do you have a highlighter or a pen or something I could borrow?”

“Yeah, okay.” I reached into the front pocket of my backpack and pulled out a mechanical pencil. “How’s this?” Suddenly I had a flash of that chart they show you in tenth-grade Sex Ed—How STDs Spread: *Billy sleeps with Kim who sleeps with Bobby who does it to Saskia who really gives it to Paul who sleeps with Holly, which makes Holly a big whore-y ho-bag who’s slept with the entire school.*

“That’s great,” said Saskia, smiling. “Thanks.”

I nodded and smiled back.

• • •

"Holly, move downstage a bit—to your left. And try your line again."

"Once more, with feeling," I deadpanned, closing my eyes and letting my head fall forward. *Gosh, I'm so clever.*

I walked downstage and shuffled sideways. "Wait—from where?"

"Start with: 'O, the more angel she, / And you the blacker devil!' And Desdemona, stay down—you're dead, remember?" Desdemona, or Rachel Bicks, who'd been sitting Indian-style on the stage sucking a Tootsie Pop, rolled her eyes and slinked back down. "Look more dead," Mr. Ballanoff barked. "Okay. Emilia, Othello. Go."

"'O, the more angel she, / And you the blacker devil!'"

"There's the spirit." Ballanoff turned toward Pete Kennedy, my scene partner, who was standing stage right holding a pillow. "Othello?"

Pete did his thing, kicking around the stage like an overzealous mummy—he was big into *gesturing* and, somehow, still, he seemed so stiff. I *blah-blahed* back, just trying to keep my words straight without flubbing my lines. I don't think we'd made it through half the scene before Ballanoff was waving his clipboard, recklessly, *suddenly*, interjecting, "God, both of you, stop, please." Then, "Holly, god, come'ere."

I walked forward. "What? What's wrong now?"

"Where's the *fire*? He's just killed someone you love, he's calling her a whore—*where's the fire*, Holly?"

I shifted back and forth from leg to leg. "I ate too much at lunch. I'm tired. We only have three more minutes of class left. . . ."

He mashed his lips together, exhaling loudly, out his nose.

Ballanoff is Jeff's age about, early forties, but I've always thought he looked older than my dad until this year when Jeff aged ten years in a blink; going from salt and pepper to stark white in three months.

"All of you," Ballanoff shouted, "Learn your lines this week. Please. Work on feeling something *other* than apathy. Next class I expect changes." He smiled then, his eyes crinkling. "You can go."

I snatched my knapsack off the auditorium floor and lunged for the door.

"Holly."

"Yes?" I whipped around.

"Help me carry this stuff, will you?"

I trudged back down the aisle, grabbing a stack of books off a chair. Ballanoff took the other stack and together we walked out the theater doors, toward his office.

"How's your dad?" he asked, balancing his papers and books between his hands and chin.

"Fine. The same."

Ballanoff knew my mom in high school. They once sang a duet together from *Brigadoon*.

"How's Nancy?" I asked. Ballanoff's wife.

"Good, thanks." He unlocked his office door, kicked an empty cardboard box halfway across the room, then dumped the pile of books onto his cluttered desk.

I set my stack down on the floor next to the door. All four corners of his office were crammed with crooked piles of books, plays, and wrinkled papers. A tiny, blue recycling bin shoved against the wall was filled to its brim with empty diet Snapple bottles.

Ballanoff sighed, walked over to the mini fridge, and took out an iced tea. "I expect more from you."

"Yeah, I know."

"It wouldn't kill you to get a little angry, or to feel something real for a change." He paused for a bit, then said, "How are you, anyways?"

"Dreamy."

"That good, huh?" He collapsed into his black pleather desk chair, swiveling from side to side.

"Oh, yeah. Pep rallies and bonfires galore. Senior year really lives up to the fantasy."

He laughed, which made me happy, momentarily. "What about you?" I asked.

"What about me?"

"You know. How's life in the teachers' lounge?"

"Oh, hey." He took a long pull off his diet iced tea. "Same old shit, year after year."

I flashed my teeth. "I love it when you swear."

"I should watch it, right? Before Harper finds out and fires me for teaching curse words alongside *Othello*." Harper. Our principal.

"It's true. Look out. You're a danger, Mr. B."

"I should hope so." He slid two fingers over the lip of his wood desk. "Thanks for your help, Holly."

I perssed the sole of my sneaker against his shiny orange door. "Anytime."

"Tell Jeff hi for me, okay?"

"Will do." I pushed backward then, out of his office and back down the hall.

"Jesus, Nils, watch the windows."

Nils was all over some dumb girl, backing her into my driver-side car door, his grubby little fingertips pressed against the glass.

"Oh. Hi Hols, hey."

"Hi. *Move*, please."

He and the girl pushed sideways so I could get my key in the lock. "Much obliged."

The girl giggled and turned toward me. *Oh, no. Not her.*

"Hey, Hols? You know Nora . . ." Nora Bittenbender. From my Calc class. Before Nils she'd supposedly slept with two teachers: David Epstein and Rick Hyde. Pretty girl but *way* bland for my taste. Fair and freckled with these jiggly, big pale boobs she was always jamming into push-up bras and too-tight tank tops. Her weight fluctuated nonstop—skinny one week, chubs the next—and her taste, Jesus, *seriously questionable.* School ensembles that bounced between cheesy nightclub clothes and oversized, heather-gray sweats. *Sexy.*

"Do you want a ride or not?" The hood of my car was covered in ash. I slid a finger through the dusty gray soot, then hopped inside. "I promised Jeff I'd take Harry out for a run after school, so either get in or I'm leaving."

"Right, yes! Okay." Nils ran over to the passenger-side door. Nora trailed him, holding on to the back of his shirt. "But could you drop Nora off on the way? She lives right by us, on Pawnee Lane."

No. "That's fine," I said. "Get in."

Nils crept into the backseat. Nora took shotgun. "Holly, thanks," she said. "I missed my bus."

"Yup."

"We have gym together, don't we?"

"Calc," I said, flooring the accelerator and, three seconds into my drive, nearly crashing into pedestrian Paul Bennett. *Good one, Holly.* I pulled to a stop and rolled down my window.

"Crap." He looked really great. He was wearing this old, thin, button-down with a small tear at the collar. His bangs lay on a diagonal across his forehead, hitting his eyes just so. "You missed me by a millimeter!"

"I'm sorry! I'm *so* sorry! Are you okay?"

Paul started toward my window, then, spotting Nils and Nora, stopped short and readjusted his backpack. "I'm fine. Just"—he waved his hands in the air and smiled—"startled, is all."

"Right. Sorry."

I watched his hair blow backward as he turned and walked on toward his car. Then I lightly pushed down on the gas and rolled out onto the main road.

"I didn't even know you knew Paul Bennett." Nils had scooched forward in his seat so that his face was floating somewhere over my armrest.

"I don't, not really."

"You sure? 'Cause he seems to know you."

I felt something un-nameable tickle my gut. Regret? Longing? I shook my head. "I mean, we have a class together. He knows my name, I guess."

"Maybe he likes you," said Nora, poking me in the shoulder.

Nils scoffed. "No offense, but, I don't think Holly's really Paul Bennett's type."

"What's that supposed to mean?" I turned sideways and gave Nils the icy eyeball. "What's Paul Bennett's type? Please! Pray tell."

Nils folded a stick of cinnamon gum into his mouth. "You know, blond. Willowy. WASPy. The anti-Holly."

"Saskia Van Wyck," said Nora, nodding.

I rolled my eyes. "Of course. Saskia Van Wyck, the anti-Holly."

"That's a good thing, Hols. She's plain spaghetti." He looked at me lovingly. "No sauce."

Nora twisted around in her seat so that she was facing Nils. "Can I have a piece of that?" She was biting Nils on the neck and pulling on his pack of gum. "I *love* cinnamon. I do."

We spent the next twenty minutes stuck in traffic on the PCH. In my rearview I watched Nils make eyes at Nora. *He's better looking than her, smarter than her, he's just better,* I thought. They were mismatched. Like fast food and fancy silverware. Or spray cheese and sprouted bread.

"Oh, hey! This is me. I'm up here, on the left," she said, "the green one with the tree." There was a porta potty parked on her front lawn next to a tall stack of aluminum siding. "We're expanding the kitchen. And adding a half-bath."

I turned up her steep driveway and stopped ten feet short of the garage. She kissed Nils on the mouth. *Smooch, smooch.*

"Thanks again, Holly." And then, to Nils, "Call me."

"Will do."

She was gone.

I kicked the car into reverse and started backing up. "Okay, get up here. I am not your chauffeur." Nils scooched from back to front, contorting to get through the tiny space between seats. We were side by side now. Neither one of us talking. I drove quickly back down Nora's twisty street and out onto the main road, where we passed my favorite rock. White and long and crater-faced; like a slice of the moon.

"Okay. What the hell, Nils, *Nora Bittenbender*?"

"So cute."

"Of course. *Cute.* What beats cute?" I snipped.

"Boobs."

"Right . . . of course. *Boobs* beats cute." I glared at him sideways. He had his head turned and tilted back, his hand hanging languidly out the window.

"You don't even know the girl, Holly."

This thing with Nils and girls started junior year with Keri Blumenthal, a pool party, and a stupid green bikini. Then before I could blink, my friend was gone and in his place was this dumb dude who *loved* Keri Blumenthal and lame bikinis and even though I'm *loath* to admit it, this is when things really changed for us. Keri Blumenthal wedged a wall between us. Fourteen days they lasted and still, when they went bust, that dumb wall stayed intact. "She talks like a baby," I said.

"Holly."

"And why does she wear those clothes?"

"Comfort . . . social conventions . . ."

"Not *any* clothes, pervert. Those *particular* clothes."

"Holly. Come on."

"Seriously, what's the deal with her and Epstein? Is that for reals, or no?"

"I dunno . . ."

"I just don't understand why you like her. You're better than—"

"Holly." He sat up really quick and grabbed my hand. "Stop it. Okay?" He tightened his grip and creepy tingles rolled up my arm. "I'm not gonna marry the girl."

I looked back at the road, mimicking Nora's babyish lilt. "You're not?"

Nils dropped my hand. "You're a weirdo, Holly."

I pursed my lips. "At least I'm not a baby with . . . big boobies."

"Weirdo."

I slapped him hard on the arm and turned up my driveway. We both laughed.

I parted ways with Nils and beelined for the fridge. Harry was at my heels begging for food, so I unwrapped a single slice of American-flavored soy cheese, rolled half into a little ball, and dropped the other half on the floor. He inhaled the thing in two seconds flat, not even stopping to chew.

I walked to my bedroom, simultaneously nibbling on my little ball of fake cheese and taking off my clothes, item by item. I slipped on my running shorts and a tank, grabbed Harry's leash, and poked my head into Jeff and Mom's room on my way to the back door. She'd been gone six months and somehow, the entire place still smelled like her: rose oil and castile soap. I don't know how that happens, someone dies and their scent stays behind. Jeff hadn't changed a thing. All her clothes were still on their racks in the closet, her perfume on the vanity, her face creams and make up in the little bathroom off their bedroom. Most days it was easy to pretend she was still around. Out at the store. On a walk. In the garden. Out with Jeff.

So I took the dog out running. Up the canyon, past Ms. Penn's place with that wicker chair she has tied to a rope so it hangs from her tree like a swing; up Pawnee Lane, past Nora Bittenbender's, past Red Rock Road, and out into town. I bought a ginger ale at the Nature Mart and walked back most of the way, trying to keep twigs and rocks out of Harry's mouth.

Later that night, around seven, Jeff came home.

"Hi, Dollface." He kissed my forehead and took a bottle of seltzer out of the fridge. He held it to his neck, then took a long swig, settling into his favorite wooden chair. "What's for dinner?"

"Tacos, maybe? I was thinking I'd drive down to Pepe's. Another night of pasta, I just might hurl."

Jeff laughed his sad little Jeff laugh and kicked off his

loafers. "'Kay, sounds good to me, whatever you want." Then he handed me a twenty. I put Harry in the car because he loves hanging his head out the window at night while I drive, and we sped down the hill, to the beach, to Pepe's, where I bought eight tacos: four potato, two fried fish, two chicken. I kept the warm white bag in my lap on the drive back, away from Harry, and thought about Mom for a second or two. Specifically, her hair: long and thick and dark, like mine. I sang along to a song on the radio I didn't really know the words to, and when my cell rang, I checked the caller ID but I didn't pick up. I didn't recognize the number.

Jeff and I ate in front of the TV that night, watching some cheesy dating reality show that he loves and I hate, but I humor him because he's my dad and his wife is dead and anything that makes him happy now, I'm into. So we finished dinner, I kissed him good night, and then I went out back to The Shack with my cell to listen to the message from my mystery caller. "Hi, Holly," said the voice on my voice mail, "it's Paul. Bennett. I'm just calling to see what you're up to tonight. Gimme a ring." *Click.* My heart shot up to my throat. We'd never talked on the phone. In fact, we'd never really talked.

I held the phone to my chest and considered calling back, I did, but the whole sex-in-his-car-at-the-beach thing had really struck me as a one-time deal. I called Nils instead.

"Hello?"

"It's me."

"You out back?"

"Yeah. Jeff's asleep in front of the TV and I'm bored."

"Be right there. I'm bringing CDs, though, okay?"

"Whatever you say." I flipped my phone shut.

"Holly-hard-to-get. Hi."

Paul and I were standing shoulder to shoulder outside my Chem class. He was wearing a battered old pair of khaki cut-offs, black aviators, and a brash grin. "You don't return phone calls?"

I stared at him, mystified, as he shuffled backward. I shook my head.

"Too bad." He blinked. "What do you have now, Chem?"

"Mm," I managed.

"You stoked?"

"What for?"

"Class." He cocked his head sideways, scanning my face for signs of humor, no doubt. "I'm kidding."

I looked at him blankly. Why were we standing there, talking still?

"Holly?"

"Hmm?"

"Are you okay?"

"I'm fine, yeah. Tired, I guess."

"Well . . . are you busy later?"

I nodded *yes I'm busy, sorry, can't hang out* and watched,

rapt, as he swung his pretty head from side to side. "I don't get you," he said.

I hugged the door frame as a couple of kids tried squeezing past me. "What's to get?" I asked, because seriously, *what's to get?* I was baffled, *really* perplexed by his sudden and obsessive interest in me. I wore ratty Levi's and dirty Chuck Taylors to school every day. I rarely brushed my hair. I had *one* friend besides my dog, and spent nights with my checked-out dad in front of the TV. What about me could possibly hold Paul's interest?

He flashed me one last look, gliding a hand along the wall, then disappearing into a crowd of kids in flip-flops and jean shorts standing around in a big square pack.

Was this some big joke or was I suddenly irresistible? Did I even *like* Paul? Did Paul truly like me? I peeled myself away from the door frame, turned a quick pivot, and shuffled into class.

Nils had his elbows pressed against the black Formica desktop and was fidgeting with some metal contraption with a long, skinny rod. I dropped my books down next to him. "What's that?"

"It's a Bunsen burner." Nils considered me. "What's wrong with you?" He moved sideways, making room. "You look pinched."

I grabbed a stool, dropped my bag to the floor, and plopped down next to him. "Just, no. Just—" I ran a finger over a crooked little heart that had been etched into the side of the desk. "Why Nora? Like, why go after her? Do you like her even?"

"Yeah, sure thing."

"No but, do you *like her* like her?"

"I like her enough." *Ick.* This sort of thing was classic *New Nils*-speak. Nils *post* Keri Blumenthal. Yes, maybe he'd had some experience this past year, and yeah, maybe I hadn't even gone past kissing with anyone pre-Paul . . . *still,* that didn't give Nils the right to be cagey and smug when I needed real, straightforward answers.

"What does that mean?"

Nils looked at me. He shrugged. "She's a nice way to pass the time."

I flinched. "Oh. Duh, of course." Then I opened my Chem book to the dog-eared page and pretended to read. So that was it. Sex. A way for Paul Bennett to pass the time. *Holly-pass-time. Holly-ho-bag.* I pressed my forehead to the crease in my textbook.

"What're you doing?"

"Resting."

"What do you care about Nora Bittenbender, anyway?"

"I don't."

"You sure you're okay?"

I sat up. "I'm fine." I gestured toward the Bunsen burner. "Come on. What the hell are we doing with this thing, anyway?"

"We're making s'mores," said Nils, pulling a misshapen Hershey's Kiss from his pocket and a crushed packet of saltines off the neighboring desk.

"Gross," I said, smiling for real this time, feeling a smidge better. "Just gross."